INTO THE TEMPEST

THE STORM BOYS SERIES
BOOK 2

N.R. WALKER

COPYRIGHT

Cover Art: Paper & Sage
Editor: Boho Edits
Publisher: BlueHeart Press
Into the Tempest © 2023 N.R. Walker
Storm Boys Series © 2023 N.R. Walker

ALL RIGHTS RESERVED:

WARNING

Intended for an 18+ audience only. This book contains material that maybe offensive to some and is intended for a mature, adult audience. It contains graphic language, and adult situations.

TRADEMARKS:

All trademarks are the property of their respective owners.

AUTHOR NOTE

This series is strictly fiction. Actual bureaus of meteorology do not work like this in real life. The author is very aware.

There has been creative licence taken in regards to weather tracking, prediction systems, and any/all meteorological practices mentioned herein.

It's just a fun and crazy ride intended for entertainment purposes only. Please enjoy it for what it is.

Also please note with Australian English the plural for antenna is antennas, not antennae.

And for reference, Storm Boy and Mr Percival, as mentioned in the end of this book, is from a much-loved Australian classic novel (by Colin Thiele, 1964) and movie (1976 and 2019).

Thank you for reading!

INTO THE TEMPEST

N.R. WALKER

THE STORM BOYS
SERIES – BOOK TWO

BLURB

Jeremiah Overton is now in charge of Darwin's Bureau of Meteorology, and his storm chaser boyfriend, Tully Larson, couldn't be happier. For Tully, it means watching summer storms with the love of his life, but for Jeremiah, it means relearning everything on equipment that's older than he is.

But summer storms also mean it's cyclone season. While Tully's no stranger to tropical storms and the occasional cyclone, for Jeremiah, it's a first.

As Tropical Cyclone Hazer bears down on the city, Jeremiah and Tully prepare to stay behind. Jeremiah knows what to expect, theoretically, but living through it is a different story.

If they live through it at all.

CHAPTER ONE
TULLY

I was nervous waiting for Jeremiah's plane to land.

Two weeks after being at the Darwin Bureau of Meteorology, he'd made a quick trip back to Melbourne to collect some of his personal belongings, pack up his apartment, and clear out his desk at work.

One night.

He'd been gone for one night and I missed him like crazy. How he'd turned my life upside down in a matter of just a few weeks I'd never know. The first week at the bunker in Kakadu had been awesome, and the two weeks helping him get his new office into some kind of workable space had been fun. But gettin' to watch afternoon storms with him, havin' him in my home, and in my bed had been the very best two weeks of my life.

I was besotted with this man, and I was nervous as hell waiting for him. Nervous that he'd get off the plane and tell me he wasn't staying, that he'd be goin' back to his old life in Melbourne. That his life was there and not here with me.

I was nervous that he wouldn't get off the plane at all.

I'd spoken to him this mornin' when he was on his way to the airport, but a lot coulda happened between then and now, and maybe he'd realised that this was all too much too soon. Maybe he didn't want to pack up his entire life and move five thousand kilometres away.

Maybe he didn't feel the same about me as I felt about him.

I was just about ready to puke by the time his flight landed. I noticed a few familiar faces in the terminal and a guy I knew from the bank made an attempt at small talk as he waited for someone to deplane as well.

"Everything okay?" he asked, glancing from me to where people were coming in through the Arrivals door.

"Oh, yeah," I mumbled distractedly. "Sure, just waitin' . . ."

Waitin' for him not to show. Waitin' for him to break my heart.

He'd nodded and, thankfully, said nothing else. His person arrived, and they left smilin' and as happy as could be. Everyone else came in greeting their familiar faces, their loved ones, their people. All smiles and hugs and laughter.

And no Jeremiah.

The doors closed and people wheeled out their luggage, leaving my stomach in knots, my heart thumping and heavy. My chest felt all too tight, and that nervousness from before was quickly becoming a sinking realisation that Jeremiah hadn't got on his flight.

He didn't want me. He didn't love me . . .

"Please be careful with that," a familiar voice said as airport staff wheeled through a cart with two large black crates. Jeremiah was ushering alongside them, frantic and frazzled.

And fucking gorgeous.

The tight band around my chest let up and, just like that, I could breathe.

"Hey," I yelled, making them stop, and in a few quick strides, I collected Jeremiah in a crushing hug, surprising him and the man pushin' the cart.

"Oh," Jeremiah squeaked, red faced and flustered, now for a whole other reason. "Tully, what are you . . . ?"

"I missed you," I blurted out, squeezin' him tight. "And I didn't see you get off the plane. I thought you mighta decided not to come back. I'm so happy to see you."

He pulled back, seemingly confused by this. "I told you I was coming back just this morning. Actually, my employer insisted I take this job. I wasn't allowed to *not* come back here; I believe that was the term they used."

Laughing, I cupped his face and pulled him in for a quick kiss. His magnificent blue eyes widened.

"Tully," he hissed.

I just grinned at him. I didn't give a fuck what people thought. I wanted to kiss him, so I did. "Need help with your gear?"

With his hand to his forehead, still flustered, he blinked a few times. "Ummm."

"You okay?"

"You befuddled me."

"Befuddled?" I threw my head back and laughed. "God, I missed you."

He scowled at me, then gestured absently to his crates and to the guy who'd been pushin' the cart, who was now looking at anyone but us. "This should be fine, but if you could take one of my suitcases . . ."

He glanced uncomfortably over at the few straggling travellers, some who were now watching us.

I got the feeling they'd never seen two men kiss before, so I grinned at them too as I collected Jeremiah's luggage. "Come on, *babe*, let's go home," I said, extra loud for our audience's benefit.

Jeremiah rolled his eyes and grumbled as we walked out. "Did you need to be so obvious?"

Yes, I did.

So, for good fuckin' measure, I pushed him up against the side of my Range Rover and kissed him properly. He resisted for half a second . . . until he didn't. He groaned as I sucked on his tongue.

I pulled back, leaving him dazed and flushed, then booped him on the nose with my finger. "I missed you."

"Don't be ridiculous," he mumbled, trying not to smile. "I've been gone one day."

"Thirty-five hours, to be exact." Not that I was counting.

The blush on his cheeks deepened, and he chewed on his bottom lip. "Should we go home then?"

Hell yes, we should.

I loaded his gear into my car, cranked up the air conditioning, and we headed out of the carpark.

"I very quickly forgot how hot it is here," he said, wiping his brow with the back of his hand. "The humidity, jeez."

"Did you get everything sorted?"

He nodded. "Brian had already boxed up my desk, so that took exactly one minute. There was no love lost there, I can assure you. They're as glad to see the back of me as I am to see theirs."

"I'm sorry."

"I'm not."

I reached over and took his hand. "It's their loss."

"My parting words were something similar."

I laughed but then asked something more serious. "And your dad?"

"He was fine," he said with a shrug. "Wished me luck. I took him out for dinner last night, like a farewell, I suppose. He said it was a waste of money."

Oh man.

I squeezed his hand. "I'm sorry."

"He appreciated the fridge and lounge I gave him though. Mine were newer than his by a decade or two." He tried to smile but it didn't quite work.

I lifted his hand to my lips and kissed his knuckles. I hated that no one in his Melbourne life was happy for him. "I'm glad you're here."

He watched me for a long moment. "I'm glad I'm here too. Did I miss a great storm last night?"

I grinned at him. "It was kinda lame. Or maybe that was just because I didn't get to watch it with you."

He rolled his eyes and looked out his window, but I could tell by his cheeks that he was smiling. "Oh," he said, as if he'd just remembered. "The heart-rate monitor you suggested? The chest strap that sports people wear?"

I think I liked where this was going . . . "Yeah?"

He cleared his throat. "I may have bought one."

I grinned. "Oh hell yes. Now we just need one of those brain monitor things, so next time you try and get struck by lightning, we can get some proper readings."

He sighed. "I don't *try* to get struck—" He stopped talking and shook his head, not even bothering to finish that sentence. "I also inquired about helmets that perform non-invasive medical imaging of the brain, because I did some research while I was stuck in traffic. There is a relatively new device that employs near-infrared light to determine the relative concentration of haemoglobin in the brain, via differences in the light absorption patterns. Because, well, most non-invasive brain scanning systems use continuous-wave spec-troscopy, where the tissue is irradiated by a constant stream of photons. However, these systems cannot differentiate between scattered and absorbed photons. But this new one—"

"Okay, I'm just gonna stop you right there," I said, putting my hand up. "And remind you who you're talkin' to. You're really gonna have to dumb all that down for me." I gave him the smile he liked best. "Or just say it's one of those helmet thingies with the white sticky pads."

He kinda winced. "Well, it doesn't have white sticky pads . . . Anyway, they're incredibly expensive, so unless I can obtain some kind of study grant, which is highly unlikely given the nature of the experiment, it's not likely I'll be purchasing one any time soon."

I reached over and squeezed his hand. "But you got the proper heart-rate monitor thingy?"

He smiled. "Yes."

My phone rang, Bluetooth putting it through the stereo system. My brother's name came on the dash screen.

I hit Answer. "Hey, butt nugget."

"Hey, nut sac."

Jeremiah's eyes widened and I laughed. "You're on speaker, and Jeremiah's in the car."

"Ah, the mystery man who's been keeping you busy."

Jeremiah's eyes almost bugged out of his head, and with a grin, I squeezed his hand. "What do you want, Ellis? We're heading home."

"Well, I'm glad you're in the car. It'll save you a trip."

"What for?"

"I need you to come to the office."

"Can't it wait till tomorrow? I'm back in the office tomorrow at eight."

"Nope. You need to sign off on the Goyer account. Shipment leaves at twenty-two hundred today."

I groaned.

"Quit your bitching," he said. "You're already in the car so you're, what? Five minutes away?"

"Hey, Ellis," I said flatly.

"If you're gonna tell me to eat a bag of dicks, I'll leave that up to you."

I snorted. "Believe me, if they sold 'em in bags, I would."

He laughed. "You're so gross."

"You started it."

"See ya when you get here. Oh, and Jeremiah," Ellis said. I could hear the smile in his voice. "Tell me, does Tully—"

I hit End Call so damn fast I hurt my finger. "Sorry about that," I said. "Whatever he was about to say was going to be embarrassing and more than likely rude."

He smiled at me. "Would you really eat dicks from a bag?"

Laughing, I changed lanes and headed toward the depot. It really wasn't far, and now that it was about to happen, the idea of Jeremiah meeting Ellis kinda gave me a thrill. We'd been so busy at his new office, and in the bedroom, everythin' else just kinda got ignored.

"This won't take more than a minute or two," I said, pulling into the depot yard. I lowered my window and slowed down at the gate, waved through when the security guard saw it was me.

Jeremiah stared at the cargo ships and the shipping containers, and at the famous knight logo. Then he turned to me, stunned. "This is you?"

"Nope, this is my mum and dad's business. I just work here."

"But this is . . . you never said you were one of Australia's major freighting companies."

I snorted. "It's just work to me." I drove up to the admin building and into my parking spot, then shut off the engine. "Come on inside. It won't take a minute."

He looked horrified. "You want me to come in with you?"

"Sure. I know you've been travellin' all day, but you can meet Ellis, and then you can confirm, once and for all, that I'm by far the better-looking brother." I grinned for good measure. "If you could say that to his face, that'd be great. If you don't mind, that is."

I got out and went to his side of the car and opened his door for him. "Come on, he won't bite. He'll be on his best behaviour, I promise." I waited for him to get out of the car, closed the door, and slung my arm over his shoulders as we walked toward the main building. "If he's not, I'll kick his arse."

"You wish you could kick my arse."

I stopped in my tracks and pulled Jeremiah to a stop with me, my arm around his shoulders falling to his waist . . .

Because there, now standin' in a neat little welcoming line at the front of the building, was Ellis—wearing a shit-eating grin.

And my parents.

I was gonna kill my brother.

CHAPTER TWO

JEREMIAH

When Tully stopped walking, I knew something was wrong. He'd stopped dead, his arm fell from my shoulders, and his fingers gripped my waist.

There were three people waiting for us, it would seem. The reason Tully froze.

One man, maybe early thirties, who looked a great deal like Tully. Only he was wearing suit pants and a shirt, and his blond hair was short.

But his grin was exactly the same.

And an older couple. Maybe fifties or sixties, well-dressed, and smiling. She was pretty, with blonde hair tied up in a twist, wearing a pantsuit. And he was a tall, solid man, with silver hair but very familiar brown eyes, and that grin . . .

Oh.

Oh boy.

"Mum," Tully said. "Dad. I wasn't expecting you . . ." Then his voice dropped. "Ellis. You scheming, festy ball sac."

Ellis laughed and leaped onto Tully in a tackle and they wrestled like teenagers. Tully's father laughed, and his mother sighed loudly. She ignored them and aimed right for me.

"Hello, dear," she said, walking toward me. "Please ignore the heathens. I tried to raise them right." She held out her hand. "I'm Brielle, Tully's mother."

Oh my god.

So this was happening.

I remembered my manners and shook her hand. "Hello. It's very nice to meet you, if somewhat unexpected. Please excuse my clothes. I've been travelling all day. If I'd have known I'd be meeting you—"

Tully was back beside me, his arm firmly around my waist again. "Mum, this is Doctor Jeremiah Overton. Jeremiah, this is my mum."

She blinked in surprise at my title. "How lovely to meet you."

Then Tully turned me to face his father. "This is my dad, Ken." And his brother, whose shirt now looked decidedly dishevelled. Had Tully ripped the collar? "And the walking, talking nut sac, Ellis."

His dad shook my hand. "Ignore them. It's nice to meet you."

Ellis gave Tully another shove and shook my hand too. "So you do exist. I thought for sure he'd made you up."

Oh, goodness.

"I do exist, yes."

"And you spent time out in the cell block with him?"

"The cell block . . ."

"He means the bunker," Tully explained.

"Oh, right. Yes. I loved it. I'd actually like to spend more time there."

"Oh, so you're as batshit crazy as he is," Ellis said, trying to touch Tully's face. Tully wrestled with him again until their mother spoke.

"Boys!"

They stopped immediately, but Mrs Larson took my arm. "Come inside out of this dreadful heat," she said, ushering me in toward the door.

I turned back to see Tully's father give them both a clip behind the ears. It didn't help that he was smiling when he did it.

"Holy shit, he's got the bluest eyes I've ever seen," Ellis said. I think it may have been an attempt to whisper but we all heard it.

"Shut the fuck up," Tully said, putting him in another headlock.

"Forgive those two," his mother said as we entered the building. "They get like that when they haven't seen each other for a while."

It was an easy twenty degrees cooler inside, and I almost sagged with relief.

"We'll go through to the cafeteria," she said. "Can I offer you a drink? Did you say you'd been travelling?"

"Ah, yes. I've come back from Melbourne."

"Oh, you must have been up early," she said, frowning. "Help yourself to whatever food you want."

"I'm fine," I tried. But wow. It was an actual cafeteria, and there were some guys in blue overalls at one table. I assumed them to be dock workers.

"We offer all our workers meals around the clock," Mrs Larson explained, clearly reading my curiosity for what it was. She led me to the beginning of the cafeteria line, slid a tray over, and loaded up a plate of sandwiches, some cut fruit, and two coffees. She took the tray to a table and sat down, and seeing Tully was in the line with his brother and father—and not really knowing what else to do—I sat opposite Mrs Larson.

She took one of the coffees and put the food in front of me. "Please, eat," she said. "Travelling is a beast, and airport food is terrible. These are made fresh all day long."

I wasn't sure what to say. "Uh, thank you." I picked up a small triangle of ham, cheese, and tomato sandwich and bit into it. It was really very good.

"So," Mrs Larson said. "You're a doctor?"

Oh great.

By the time I'd finished chewing and swallowing, Tully had plonked himself down next to me. "He has a PhD in meteorological sciences," he said, with his mouth half full of what was possibly chocolate cake.

"Not a medical doctor," I added. "Much to my father's disdain."

I hadn't meant that to sound so bitter, but anyway, there it was.

"Don't let him fool ya," Tully said. "He's humble and self-deprecating, but he's a genius, and at least ten years ahead of his colleagues."

I looked at Tully then, because that was such a weird

thing to say . . . and he smirked at me with a hint of daring in his eyes. And something that looked like pride?

I wasn't sure. I wasn't familiar with it. My face flamed, nonetheless. "Uh, I think genius is a stretch."

Tully laughed and, to my utter horror, put his hand to my jaw and thumbed my cheek. His brown eyes, kind and warm. "Whatcha blushing for?"

Oh.

My.

God.

I went so red and my cheeks burned so hot I was sure it could only be measured in kelvin. I could even feel it in my hairline. I pulled his hand away, giving him a 'your parents are right there' look, and what did he do?

He laughed.

His hand fell to my thigh, and he kept it there, giving my leg a squeeze. My throat was suddenly feeling a little tight, so I sipped my coffee and dared to glance at Tully's parents and brother.

They were all looking at Tully. His dad was smiling at him, though clearly surprised. His brother was staring at him as if he'd sprouted a second head, and his mother was looking at him fondly.

At least they weren't looking at me. I ate more sandwich and pretended this whole encounter wasn't mortifying.

"So, Jeremiah's now in charge of the Darwin office," Tully said, still singing my praises, which I wasn't used to—at all. "He's staying with me."

Oh my days.

He just told them we were cohabitating. Not even that I was staying at his house, but rather that I was staying *with him.*

As in, not leaving. Not returning to Melbourne. I was *with him.*

I let out a long, slow, somewhat shaky breath. "Well, the position was thrust upon me."

Oh . . .

Did I just use the words position and thrust upon me in one sentence?

To his parents? And his brother?

I wanted to die.

Was it possible for the floor to open up and swallow me whole? Maybe I could choke on a grape.

I tried. No luck.

Tully chuckled beside me, his face far too close to mine. "You okay there?" he whispered.

"No. Is a sinkhole not too much to ask for?"

He laughed and kissed my shoulder, then pulled me to my feet. "Okay, we're gonna get going."

"Oh, did you sign whatever needed signing?" I asked. I hadn't noticed him doing that, but this had all been such a whirlwind.

"No." Tully glared at his brother. "Ellis was bullshitting me. This was an ambush."

Ellis grinned. "Just wanted to see if you actually existed, sorry. And to embarrass Tully. Given Mum and Dad were both in the office, it was perfect timing."

"Oh."

All right then.

Tully grumbled. "After travellin' ten thousand kilometres in two days, he had to pack up his apartment, maybe grab a few hours' sleep to make it back to the airport in time this morning, fly for half a day, only to get here and meet my family without any warning." He put his arm around me. "Jeremiah has every right to be pissed at you, Ellis."

Oh my . . . "Uh, no, it's fine," I said quickly.

Tully nudged me. "No, be pissed at him."

I shook my head. "No, no. It's fine."

Ellis stood up. "I'm sorry."

I shrank back into Tully and gave him pleading eyes. "I said it's fine."

"Why won't you yell at him," Tully urged. "Lay on the guilt. Make him suffer."

Oh god.

This was all a ploy to chide his brother.

I smiled at Mr and Mrs Larson. "Thank you for the food and coffee. It was very nice to meet you." And then Ellis. "And you, as well. But yes, I should get going. I need to check in at the office this evening."

Tully slung his arm over my shoulders, not before giving his brother the bird, and led me to the door. "Why didn't you rip him a new one?" he asked. "I set it up perfectly."

"Because he looks too much like you!"

Obviously, I said that too loud because Ellis laughed before the cafeteria door could shut, and Tully gave him another bird before leading me out and into the car.

I sat in the seat, and Tully closed my door. I couldn't believe what had just happened. I couldn't get my thoughts together. Apparently, all I could do was stammer at Tully as he got in behind the wheel.

"Wh-wh-what the . . . I just . . . just met . . . oh my god. Those were your parents!"

Tully's annoyingly breathtaking grin lit up his whole stupidly handsome face. "Okay, first up, I had no idea. That was all Ellis' doing. So, I'm sorry for blindsiding you. Not my intention at all." He sat back in his seat, still smiling, far too pleased with himself. "But ya know what? I ain't mad about it."

"I can see that."

"I thought it went well."

"I said the words *position* and *thrust upon* in the same sentence, Tully. To their faces."

He laughed. "Pretty sure they like you."

"I've never met anyone's parents before!"

He shot me a look. "Well, fair's fair. I've never introduced anyone to my parents before."

I stared at him. "I'm the first? Because that bestows a whole lot of added pressure I didn't need right now. Oh my god, Tully, they must think I'm . . ." I gestured to my been-travelling-all-day clothes and hair. "I look like a homeless man."

"You look perfect."

I sighed, my hand to my forehead, unable to process . . .

"Hey, Jeremiah. Look at me," he murmured softly. I did, and his smile softened as he studied my face for a long second. "I'm glad it was you."

"Pardon?"

"I'm glad you were the first to meet my folks. As my boyfriend."

Boyfr . . .

Boyfriend . . .

I squeaked. "What?"

He chuckled, leaned right across me, and pulled my seatbelt. Our faces were an inch apart, his eyes alight. "Boyfriend." He buckled me in, the click loud in the silence, and I started. "Well, we *are* living together, so . . ."

I was feeling lightheaded. "Do you . . . is that . . . maybe we . . ."

He grinned. "Nope. Boyfriends it is." He took my face in his hands, planted a soft, wet kiss on my lips, then sat back in his seat and started the engine. "Did you wanna go home first? Or straight to the office?"

My mind was a spinning wheel without the hamster. "Uh . . ."

He put the car in reverse and backed out. "Maybe we should go to the office first, because once I get you home, I don't see us leavin' for a while. If you know what I mean."

The next thing I knew we were on our way to my office. "I thought I was supposed to be the bossy one."

"You are. But you can't win all the time."

"So you can just declare us boyfriends without consulting with me?"

"Correct. What would you prefer I introduce you as?" He looked from the road to me. "Lover? Fuck buddy?"

"Oh my god, no."

"Meteorological cohabitator?"

I squinted at him.

He grinned, victorious. "See? Boyfriend it is."

I sighed, even though my heart was doing some weird palpitational dance and I was trying not to smile. "I've never had a boyfriend before."

"Me either. Or a girlfriend." Then he made a face. "Well, not really. There were some I hung out with a few times over the course of some weeks or months, but we were never . . ." He shifted in his seat. "We were never like us."

We were never like us . . .

"Like us?"

He shifted in his seat again and changed hands on the steering wheel. "Yeah. Like we are. Living together and stuff."

I got the impression that wasn't what he wanted to say.

We pulled into the yard at my Bureau of Meteorology office, and when Tully stopped the car, he gave me a smile that didn't sit quite right. "Okay, here we are," he said quickly, and got out.

I wasn't sure what that was about, but Doreen's motorbike was under the carport and I didn't want to keep her waiting.

Quite frankly, she scared me.

Tully bounded up the steps to the office and hollered, "Hey, it's us," as he disappeared inside.

I followed, bumbling into the darkened office to find Tully standing next to Doreen. Bruce, the fluffy dog, was on the chair, watching me as if I had to report in to him. Tully was grinning, Doreen was glaring. Her shirt had the Rolling Stones' mouth and tongue on it with *Lick a Lesbian* written underneath.

Nice.

"Huh," she all but grunted at me. "Surprised to see you came back."

Why did everyone think that?

"I told you I'd return," I said. "Not entirely sure why the general consensus was that I'd quit. I'm yet to quit anything. If you believe I lack the intestinal fortitude—"

She threw her head back and laughed. "I can see you got plenty-a that, kid."

I frowned at her, unsure of how to take her. "Anyway, I'm very grateful you could fill in for me and watch the fort while I squared away my old life in Melbourne."

"Well, ya gave me two weeks off," she said. "Least I could do is fill in one day for ya. Just try not to make a habit of askin'. I'm still retired, just not dead yet."

I nodded, almost bowing to her. "Thank you."

She clapped me on the shoulder, hard enough to make me have to counter my weight. I really needed to learn how to brace myself better. Then she scooped up Bruce and moved to the door. She pointed to the Doppler radar. "Got a tropical low moving in from Malaysia. They've had heavy falls and localised flooding. But we also got a storm cluster moving in across the Philippines. If they meet in some perfect storm scenario bullshit and swing south, and it's lookin' likely they will, shit's gonna get real bad. I've been keepin' an eye on it. Suggest you do the same."

I looked at the screen. "This front's moving directly into it?"

She gave a solemn nod. "Mm."

Well, shit. That wasn't good. "Okay, thanks."

With a gruff goodbye, she left, and a few seconds later her motorbike roared to life, and she and Bruce drove away.

"She frightens me."

Tully laughed. "Which is why you looked her right in the eye and said, 'If you think I lack the intestinal fortitude.'" He shook his head. "If that's how you react to people who scare you, I'm not surprised walkin' into a lightning storm ain't a problem for you."

I had to think about what he said, what he meant. "Was I abrasive?"

Tully, still grinning, shook his head, and with his hands to my face, pulled me in for a kiss. "You're amazing, you know that?"

"I didn't mean to sound unappreciative to her. Perhaps I should—"

"You were fine," he murmured. "I think she likes you."

"I didn't want to have to ask her to come back, even for one day."

"I know you didn't. But she didn't mind. Pretty sure if she didn't want to help out, she'd tell you." I sighed, and he pulled me close, brushing his nose to mine. "I've missed you."

"I was only gone for one day—" I began, then when his eyes met mine, I amended, "—thirty-five hours."

His smile was so serene, but then he looked around. "Well, do what you gotta do. I have plans for you tonight that don't involve bein' naked in your office. I'd rather see those plans unfold in bed and not here."

I rolled my eyes but set about getting my work done. Tully busied himself tidying up more of the shelves and packing all the old gear into boxes. He'd done most of it during my first two weeks here. He'd helped me every day, even spent his own money buying me new monitors, and he fixed a second chair he'd found in the corner.

But given there wasn't much for him to do, after only one hour, he was bored.

And horny.

He kept bothering me with sensual touches, slow neck massages, and back hugs with soft whispers in my ear.

"Please tell me we won't be here long," he murmured. "Unless you wanna do me on the control panel." He nodded toward the radars. "Not sure those switches would be too comfortable, but I'm willing to try. I don't want to wait anymore."

I could feel his excitement pressing against my arse, and when I didn't rebuke his idea, his smile became a smirk and he leaned his back against the panel board and pulled me with him.

"Where's the chest-strap monitor?" he asked, raking his hand down over my arse. "Is it in your bag in the car?"

"I'm not wearing it during sex."

He chuckled. "Oh, we absolutely *will* be using it during sex. We can take it in turns. I insist that we do." But then he pulled my hips to his and shoved his tongue in my mouth, so I couldn't argue.

I hated that it worked.

My god, he felt so good against me, and as I pushed my weight on him, he lifted one leg, hitching it around my arse. I held his face and kissed him, opening his mouth with mine, tilting our heads so I could give him more of my tongue.

He made a guttural sound that curled my insides, and he clawed at my back.

Was I really about to do this here?

At my work? On the control board?

God, I think I was . . .

How was this even my life now? Me . . . doing this, with a gorgeous man like Tully . . .

Something beeped, and he groaned. He tried to widen his legs and I pinned him against the panels, grinding against him like some horny teenager. My god, it was so unbidden. So wicked.

So hot.

Something beeped again, and he smiled against my mouth. "You're about to set me off," he said, then kissed me again, deeper, more frantic. "Gonna make me—"

It beeped again, and then again, and again, and again.

I tried to see what it was, not wanting to take my mouth from his, not wanting to stop . . .

"Is that your watch?" he asked. "Take it off."

But it wasn't my watch.

Then I saw what was beeping.

"Holy shit."

"Oh yeah," Tully breathed. "I need to get naked."

"No. Holy shit," I said, stepping back and letting him find his feet. I couldn't take my eyes off the screen. "Holy shit, Tully."

Whether he could see the seriousness in my eyes, or if it was my voice, I wasn't sure. But he followed my line of sight. "What is it?"

"That's an early detection warning."

The data reel began to spin, and more lights flashed.

"An early detection warning for what?"

I met his gaze, my heart hammering. "A cyclone."

CHAPTER THREE
TULLY

I stared at the radar. Jeremiah flipped some switches and made the beeping stop. "But that won't reach us, right? It's so far away."

Jeremiah didn't answer.

In the next few seconds, he had his phone pressed to his ear and he was searchin' on one radar while reading data on another.

I should have known then.

Nothing scared him.

But he looked kinda scared now.

I looked at the radar that had been beeping, the same one Doreen had signalled to. She'd been watching something on it, was concerned enough to mention it . . .

On the blinking radar, a massive cloud band was moving across Asia. It was sweeping southeast, carried on a warm tropical low. A massive spiral rainband, with intense rainfall extending outward from the centre. And it was now projecting a path to cross land over Darwin.

"Yes, an initial tropical cyclone alert . . . Yes, I'm aware," Jeremiah said. "If it continues to . . . That's correct, official cyclone watch . . . No, sir . . . Yes, that's correct, sir, I believe we'd be looking at a Category 5."

His eyes met mine, and I felt the blood drain from my face.

Category 5.

Jesus fucking Christ.

He ran his hand through his hair, nodded, and spoke into his phone. "I'll issue the CXML, but it'll take some time . . . because the instruments here belong in a goddamn museum."

He ended the call and tossed his phone onto the panel, then tapped the radar, his eyes meeting mine.

Grim.

"Category 5?"

He nodded. "If its trajectory doesn't change. There's nothing but warm air in its path and it's just going to gain strength."

Category 5.

He gestured to another screen. "It has perfect conditions. There's nothing between there and here to stop it."

"When?" I asked. "When will it be here?"

"Five days."

"Five? That's ages. Anything can happen between now and then. Why isn't it on that radar yet?" I pointed to another screen.

"Because it's out of Australian waters. This radar"—he pointed to the really old one—"is tracking. We share feeds with the International Committee . . ."

"But it might dissipate, right? It might lose momentum, change trajectory?"

His eyes caught mine, and I could see he was trying to understand why I didn't believe him.

"It might," he allowed. "And I really hope it does. But the probability that it will continue as projected is high. We have these measures in place for a good reason, Tully. It's now an official cyclone watch. If it stays on track and reaches Australian waters, that will upgrade on day three to an alert. People need to know so they can make informed choices. Even if the cyclone downgrades, there will still be flood warnings, wind warnings, dangerous surf conditions. Severe storm warnings, rain, hail. If people want to evacuate, they can. Either way, people need to stock up on essentials and get prepared."

Again, the sincerity with which he spoke, the urgency underlined with fear, told me all I needed to know. Whatever was comin' was enough to put that edge of worry in his eyes.

I took out my phone, found the number I was after, and hit Call. "Tully," Dad answered cheerfully. "Your mother and I were just talking about you. What's up? Thought you'd be busy tonight with your new man. Gotta say, we were surprised to meet him. I know it was your brother's doing, but still, we've never met any—"

"Ah, Dad," I said. "Sorry to interrupt. I'm with Jeremiah right now. We called into his work before we went home. I know you have people who watch the weather and shit, but the bureau will be issuing an official cyclone watch. It's being sent out now."

"Is this that storm off the coast of Malaysia? Joseph's already monitoring it, and we've already changed shipping routes. You know this."

"Yeah, well, Jeremiah said it's heading our way. And I'm lookin' at a radar right now that's tellin' us Darwin will be a direct hit, Dad. And a possible Category 5 when it gets here."

There was a beat of silence and then the quiet tapping on a keyboard. "A Category 5, you said?"

Jeremiah nodded.

"Yeah, Dad. It's not good. We've got less than five days to get all the ships loaded and out of the harbour."

There was a familiar beeping of an incoming call. "That's Joseph calling me now. Christ almighty. Thanks for your call, Tull."

The line went dead, and Jeremiah gave my arm a squeeze. But then another radar started to beep, and the data screens were rolling information so fast they almost blurred.

Jeremiah was flippin' switches and reading screens like a madman. "Argh, why is everything so goddamned old?"

His phone rang again, and he was talking stats and data so fast to whoever that was, and about a minute later, a familiar motorbike came back into the yard. Doreen, with Bruce under her arm, came stomping back into the office. "I been gone for a hot minute and you issued a track map on a Cat 5? And I hear about it on the damn radio?"

He pointed to the radar screen and her face paled. "Fucking hell," she mumbled. Then she growled. "It wasn't that bad when I was in charge. What the hell are you doin' to the world?"

He shot her a glare and ignored the person he was talking to on the phone. "Like I did this," he said to her. "We need to run the CMXL."

I didn't know what that was, but she did what he asked, and then, like one single being with four arms, the two of them worked that panel together.

My hopes of takin' Jeremiah home for a night of smoking hot sex were dashed, but I didn't even mind too much. 'Cause it sure was amazing to see him at work.

Life-threatening Category 5 tropical cyclones, aside.

He was a pro. He was in charge, doing everything all at once. Takin' phone calls, makin' calls, directing information and data.

I helped where I could. I ordered them pizza for dinner. I played with Bruce. I took him out to see the storm roll in as the sun went down. And at about ten, everything had died down enough for them to stop.

"What do we do now?" I asked.

"Now we wait," Jeremiah said. "And we watch."

Doreen stretched her back. "Now we go home. You ain't gonna be sleeping much this week. Get some shuteye tonight. See ya back at six."

"You don't need to come back," Jeremiah said, standing up. "I respect your decision to retire, and quite frankly you deserve a break. You've managed this place forever on your own, and I—"

"Son, you've gotta Cat 5 on your hands. I said I'll be here at six." She whacked him on the shoulder again and he fell onto the control panel. By the time he'd collected himself, Doreen and Bruce were gone out the door.

He rubbed his arm and made a face. "Right, then."

Chuckling, I cupped his face. "Let's get you home. You've had a big day."

He nodded with a sigh. "Yes, okay."

He did what he needed to do to the control panel, we locked everything up, and went home. He was quiet on the drive, though I noticed his blinks were getting longer and slower. "Almost home," I said, taking his hand.

"Thank you for today. For the pizza. For staying with me."

"You don't need to thank me. It's what boyfriends do."

He snorted and shook his head. "I forgot about that."

I gasped, faking my horror. "How could you forget?"

"Had a busy evening."

He sure had.

"Do you think it'll hit us?"

His eyes cut to mine and he gave a nod. "Unfortunately, it looks that way. There's just nothing to pull it up. In fact, the path it's on will only make it stronger."

"Then all we can do is be prepared," I said, trying to cheer him up. "You've sent out every alert you can, you're trackin' it, satellites are monitoring for every little thing." I squeezed his hand. "Darwin learned a lot after Cyclone Tracy. New constructions all have to comply to cyclone building standards. We'll fare much better this time."

"What about the remote communities?" The corner of his mouth turned down. "What about them?"

"There'll be evacuations and they'll be moved to safer locations." I gave his hand a bit of a shake. "Jeremiah, that's not your responsibility. You've issued the alerts as soon as you could. You gave them the most notice possible. That's your responsibility, and you've done it well."

"I've never . . ." He sighed, then started again. "I've never had to issue alerts for a cyclone before. I've never been in charge before."

I slowed down for my driveway and waited for the garage door to open. "Babe, you'll do great. You've already done great. And Doreen's stickin' around. She's been through this before. You two will be the best team for the job."

I drove in, and he still hadn't said anything, so I got out and walked around to his door. "Come on, let's get you to bed."

"My gear . . ."

"Can wait." I took his hand and helped him out of the car and led him straight up the stairs to my ensuite bathroom. "You need a steaming hot shower and sleep," I said, pulling his shirt over his head and giving his nipple a tweak just for fun.

He batted my hand away and rubbed his pec. "Ow."

"Sorry. It's what boyfriends do."

He rolled his eyes and pulled off his shoes and socks as I set the shower going for him. I wasn't gonna join him, but seein' him naked and wet, with his head back and his eyes closed . . .

I stripped off and walked in after him, my hands on his hips, my dick against his arse, my lips on the nape of his neck. He groaned under the stream of water, lettin' his head fall back onto my shoulder. I took the soap and began washing his chest, his arms.

"Is this what boyfriends do?" he murmured, his voice rough.

I turned him around and pushed him against the tiles, crushing my mouth to his, cupping his balls, and stroking his erection.

He groaned into my mouth and raked his hands down my back, to my arse, and finally to my cock. We brought each other to orgasm, a mix of soap and steam and sex. And when he slumped against me, I dried him off and took him to bed.

He rested his head on my chest and his breathing was deep and even and I wrapped him my arms around him tight. He snuggled in and mumbled something I didn't quite hear.

I kissed the top of his head. "What did you say?"

"'S what boyfriends do."

I chuckled and gave him another kiss, because yeah, apparently this—being close, being affectionate, and being so damn happy—was exactly what boyfriends did.

Jeremiah was up and gone before six. He took the Jeep. Why he preferred it over the newer Rover I'd never know, but it somehow suited him. And with the house empty and the sun barely risen, I went to work early.

I'd had time off when I'd taken Jeremiah to the bunker and a few afternoons here and there over the last two weeks to help him get his office up to some kind of standard.

I knew there'd be a lot of catching up to do at the office, so heading in early was the least I could do. Plus, the imminent cyclone meant the shipping industry went into overdrive.

I'd replied to all my emails and had my first coffee by the time Dad arrived, pokin' his head through my door. "You're here early."

"Figured we'd be busy," I said.

He nodded. "Thanks for the heads-up last night. Perks of being a storm watcher, huh?"

"Well, we got to Jeremiah's office and the bureau radars started going off."

"Ah," he said. "Gotta love getting firsthand inside information." He stepped inside my office with an awkward look on his face and I knew he was about to say something about yesterday. "So, Jeremiah, huh? Your mother and I wondered why we hadn't seen much of you lately, and your brother told us you'd met someone."

I sighed, but stupidly couldn't help but smile at the mention of his name. "Yeah. Jeremiah. He's uh . . . He's kinda great."

"And he's staying with you?"

"He is. It was just supposed to be a temporary thing. Given he had no notice about takin' on the job here."

"But now it's not temporary?"

"I'd like it not to be," I admitted. "We haven't really talked about it. He just got back with some gear yesterday. We met you guys, then went straight to his office and got the cyclone warning. We didn't really have the chance to talk about much."

Had the chance to give mutual handjobs in the shower though . . .

"You really like him," Dad said. "It was good to see you happy with him yesterday. Your mum's over the moon. Finally getting to meet your . . . your . . ."

"Boyfriend."

He grinned at the confirmation.

Then, like a sudden pimple appearing, my brother Ellis walked in. "Oh, if it isn't little love-struck Tully-wully who couldn't keep his hands off his boyfriend's face yesterday."

I threw my stapler at his head. He deflected it with his arm and it hit the floor, separating into pieces. "Ow."

Dad huffed at him. "Pick that up."

He rubbed his forearm. "He threw it at me."

"You deserved it," Dad said.

Ellis sneered at me and I gave him the middle finger. He picked up the stapler and all the staples and dumped them in a pile on my desk.

Dad was back in boss mode. "Meeting at nine in the boardroom."

He left and Ellis sat down in the chair across from my desk. "So, cyclone, huh?"

I sighed. "Yeah. Jeremiah's pretty confident it'll cross land here. It might change. Hopefully it'll get downgraded."

He watched me for a second. "You really like this one, doncha."

It wasn't a question.

I nodded.

"I mean, you've had dates before, but I ain't ever seen you be all touchy-feely with 'em like you were with him."

"Shut the fuck up," I said jokingly.

He shook his head a little. "His eyes. They're so blue it's freaky."

"He's not freaky," I snapped. I wasn't joking this time. Sure, when I'd first met Jeremiah, I'd thought the same. But after getting to know him and knowing that people had called him freak and weird his whole life, I couldn't help but feel defensive.

Ellis put his hands up. "Okay, calm down." He watched me again, and if he was waiting for an apology, he wasn't getting one. "I get it. Sorry," he said. "You *really* do like this one."

"He's not a *this one*." I wasn't entirely sure if Jeremiah was *the one*, but hearing him bein' disrespected really fucking irked me. I picked up the stapler. "Unless you'd like to explain to the ER doctor how this got lodged up your arse, shut the fuck up."

Ellis grinned and sighed. "We're gonna be running

double time trying to get cargo offloaded so the ships can get back out to sea, away from the storm."

I was well-aware. "Yeah."

"Dad said you were at the bureau office when the alert went out. Must have been pretty cool."

I smiled at the memory of Jeremiah in his element, in charge. "It was, yeah."

CHAPTER FOUR
JEREMIAH

Cyclone Hazer.

When the approaching tropical storm's centre reached winds of over sixty-three kilometres per hour, it was given a name. In conjunction with the World Meteorological Organization's Regional Tropical Cyclone Committee, and given the cyclone had technically originated in Indonesia, it was named there.

Which meant I didn't get to allocate the name.

And for that, I was grateful.

I didn't want the responsibility of that. I felt bad enough that I'd been the one to initiate the warning alerts.

Sure, it was exciting and probably what most meteorologists dreamed of, but the danger was real. And knowing it was coming . . .

It wasn't so much excitement as it was dread.

The meteorological world was abuzz with the news, but I didn't want this.

I wanted lightning and thunder. I wanted light

shows of fury and power. Not paths of death and destruction.

Knowing Doreen would be arriving at six, I made two coffees and handed one to her as she walked through the door.

She sipped her coffee and studied the radar screens. "How's it shaping up?"

"Right on track," I said. "Cyclone Hazer."

"T-minus?"

"Still at five days."

She nodded as though she knew this already. "Shit."

"Yep."

We did what needed doing for an hour—comms with the World Cyclone Committee and confirming data with the bureau head office—until Doreen stood up and collected Bruce. "Well, we may as well take shifts for the next few days; no point in us both being here all the time. I'll be back at eight tonight for the graveyard shift, and you can start at six bells tomorrow. How does that sound?"

She didn't wait for me to answer. With another whack to my shoulder, she was gone.

"Sounds great, thanks," I said to the empty room.

Because it *was* a good idea. I was grateful for her being here at all. And while my name was now atop hers on the boss list, we both knew who was calling the shots.

I didn't mind.

It wasn't a power grab. This was an impending natural disaster. It wasn't time for a pissing contest. It was time for all hands on deck and teamwork.

Plus, I liked Doreen.

I liked that she was absolutely no nonsense, no bull-shit. A very far cry from my old colleagues in Melbourne. And when this cyclone was over and she went back to retirement, I might even miss the company.

I thought I'd like being on my own. In Melbourne, I'd basically worked on my own anyway, and given this post was a one-person job, I was expecting to be solo.

But since I'd started, I'd had Tully with me almost every day, sorting out the office, updating the two old box screens above the dash to flatscreen TV's, and getting familiar with the old dashboard itself. Then I'd had Doreen come to help, and . . . for the first time in my career, I'd actually had a co-worker that I liked, that I trusted. That I respected, and who respected me.

It was a nice change, and it reinforced that I'd made the right decision in being here.

Just after nine that morning, a white van pulled into the yard. At first I thought it was a storm-chasing van with the radar and aerials on top, but then I saw the small news logo on the door.

Great.

A woman with a terrible jacket and a microphone got out, followed by the driver who, as it turned out, was also the cameraman. I met them at the door, not knowing what to do or say and wishing to god Doreen was still here. Though the shirt she'd worn today—with a cute cat licking its paw and the words *I lick pussy* on it—would need blurring out on TV, but at least it wouldn't have been me . . .

"Can I help you?" I asked, coming down the steps to meet them.

"Lindsey Ashley, Channel 4," she said in that voice newsreaders used. "We'd like to speak to someone about the latest cyclone warning and perhaps what our viewers can expect over the next coming days."

"Ah . . ." Dear god. "Well, that'd be me, I guess. I'm the only one here."

"And you are?"

"Doctor Overton, meteorologist. However, I'm sure you can appreciate my time is best spent elsewhere." I gestured back to the door. "This office is run manually, and I have a lot going on right now."

"I won't keep you long," she said, as if I didn't have a choice in it.

The cameraman moved to get a better angle, which was apparently closer.

A lot closer.

"And we're rolling," he murmured.

"Doctor Overton joins us from the Darwin Bureau of Meteorology. We thank you for your time, I understand you're incredibly busy. We believe the initial warning alert came from this office."

The camera trained in on me.

I tried not to be a rabbit in headlights. I kept my eyes on her and not on the camera, cursing Doreen for not being here, with her crude shirt and yappy dog.

And her baseball bat.

"Ah, yes, that's correct," I said.

"What can you tell us about the approaching storm? Cyclone Tracy devastated Darwin in 1974, and the horrors of that are still fresh in the minds of many Darwinians. Will we see a repeat of Cyclone Tracy?"

Don't cause panic, don't cause panic. Just be factual.

"Tracy was a Category 4, and Hazer is shaping up to be a Category 5. The last Cat 5 we saw was Ita, which devastated parts of far north Queensland, though Ita crossed land as a Cat 4 in an unpopulated area and deflected. Hazer is expected to make direct contact with Darwin as a Category 5. We will see rainfalls of anywhere up to five hundred mils, which will cause flooding, and destructive winds of up to two hundred and twenty kilometres per hour. I'm assured there have been construction changes since the seventies to better withstand such destruction, however I would urge all residents to listen to emergency services and police. If you're issued an evacuation order, please heed those warnings. There will likely be disruptions to essential services, so be prepared; stock up on food and water, ensure the safety of any elderly folks in your life and any pets. And if you are able to leave, I would suggest you do so."

She stared at me before blinking a few times, seemingly to collect her thoughts. "That's a grim warning," she said.

I wasn't sure which parts of what I'd said she didn't understand. Was I supposed to sugar-coat it?

"Is there any chance the cyclone will change course?"

I resisted sighing and managed a nod instead. "As with any calculations regarding weather, there is always a chance, and I'll be very happy to be proven wrong in this case. But as it stands now, we can expect the storm to begin its approach with torrential rain and strong wind gusts. Hazer is on track to hit Darwin in the morning five days from today. Any changes will be updated as they happen, and the public will be notified as a priority."

A radar started to beep inside and I took that as my cue. "Thank you for your time," I said, making it up two steps before she stopped me.

"Doctor Overton," she said. "Can you tell us what to expect?"

I thought I already had.

"We've had other cyclone warnings in Darwin before," she said, "that never amounted to much, and there tends to be complacency—"

Out of patience, I looked straight at the camera. "This will be a *significant* weather event. Listen to emergency service announcements. If you don't need to be here, don't be here."

I turned then and went inside, locking the door behind me. I didn't have time to dwell on how badly that interview had gone because for the few next hours I had more data, more comms with other agencies, and no time to be concerned with second-rate reporting.

Another news van pulled into the yard, a man in a suit this time knocked on the door, and I ignored them.

And then my phone began to ring with unknown numbers. How they got my number, I'll never know. I could only assume they got my name from the interview I'd done earlier . . . The first few callers claimed to be with some news channels I'd not heard of—which I declined to comment for—and after a while, I switched my phone to silent.

After that, in my little dark office, doing a dozen things at once, I completely lost track of time. It wasn't until a familiar Range Rover pulled into the yard that I checked my watch. It was after six. But then a not-familiar man got out of the car.

I did a double take on the security camera.

I mean, he was familiar.

But oh boy, did he look different.

Tully took the steps two at a time and I dashed to unlock the door before he could try to open it. I swung the door inward and looked him up and down. "Uh, hello, stranger," I said. "While you *are* incredibly gorgeous, I won't be buying anything you're selling as I already have a boyfriend."

His smile quirked upward, confused. "What?"

I gestured to his suit pants, lace-up shoes, and crisp white button-down shirt, his hair pulled back into a small ponytail. "Who are you and where is the Tully who wears old clothes and no shoes?"

He rolled his eyes. "I told you I wear proper clothes to work. Do you not like it?"

I glanced down at how his shirt was tucked in at his narrow waist, how the column of his neck looked against the open collar. His hair . . . pulled back. "Oh yes. As I said, gorgeous. But I like the shorts with the rip in them and the threadbare shirt just as much."

He grinned, and his voice dropped to a sultry whisper. "And I like it when you turn down handsome strangers because you have a boyfriend."

He looked at my mouth and licked his lips, stepping in for a kiss.

I pulled him in, then closed and locked the door behind him. He leaned up against the wall and pulled me against him, his hand on my hip. "My sexy and smart boyfriend was all over the news today. On the TV and everything."

Well, that was a mood killer.

"Oh god." I sighed. "Was I terrible? I wasn't expecting an interview and I hadn't prepared anything, and she asked me stupid questions. Then I had more people turn up and so many phone calls I turned my phone off."

He took my hand and studied my fingers. "I know. I called several times. I was coming to see if you were okay. I was worried."

"I'm sorry," I whispered. I cupped his face and kissed him softly. "I've been so busy."

"I assumed that was the case, but still . . . I had to come and see if you were okay." He pulled me against him again, his back against the wall, his hand snaking up from my hip to my jaw, and he brought my face in for another kiss.

A deeper kiss, open mouths and a taste of his tongue.

Damn.

He made me forget where I was, what I was supposed to be doing. I almost forgot how to breathe.

Until my stomach growled so loud it made him laugh.

"Hungry for something?" he murmured, his lips wet and swollen.

"Yes," I breathed, touching my fingertip to his bottom lip. I went to kiss him some more, but then my stomach growled again, and he held my face, his smile now gone.

"What did you eat today?"

"Oh, I uh . . ." Uh oh. "I forgot. I was busy and I . . ."

He sighed and pinched my chin between his thumb and forefinger. "You need to look after yourself," he chastised warmly. "You have to remember to eat. I know you're busy and you're stressed but, Jeremiah, you'll be no good to anyone if you're sick."

I opened my mouth to argue, because I could damn well look after myself, just as something on the console started to beep. He sighed again and squeezed my hand. "I'll be back with some dinner." He went to open the door and found it locked, giving me a puzzled look.

"Reporters and . . . just people in general, really."

He chuckled as he let himself out. "I'll be back."

I didn't remember to say thank you until he'd already gone. I wasn't used to having someone look after me, and I made a mental note to make more of an effort.

I switched off the beeping noise and uploaded the latest data to the news feed. The fact I still had to do this manually was a testament to the age of this gear, and after this cyclone, if this building still stood, I'd officially be requesting a full upgrade.

When Tully came back with a bag of takeout, he sat in

Doreen's chair and I reached over and squeezed his hand. "Thank you," I said. "I didn't mean to sound ungrateful before. I appreciate everything you do. I'm not used to having anyone look out for me, so my first knee-jerk reaction is to be defensive, and I want you to know that's not a reflection on you, but rather on myself."

He studied me for a quick second before he wheeled his chair over and gave me a quick kiss. "I know. But thank you for saying that."

"I'm very new to this, and I'm set in my ways. And I would never mean to offend you or take you for granted, so if you ever feel disrespected or unappreci-ated, please tell me. What might be glaringly obvious to other people is somewhat lost on me, and I just want you to know that." I cringed. "That you will probably have to tell me to stop every once in a while to remove my head from my arse."

"Oh, don't worry. I'll tell ya." He grinned at me. "But thank you. I know it ain't easy for you. I'm more of a let's-talk-about-our-feelings kinda guy, and the idea of doin' that makes you wanna die. I get it. There's nothin' wrong with it. It's just how we were raised."

I opened my mouth to argue that point, but every-thing he'd said was the truth.

He shrugged. "So I just hafta be extra mushy with you until you're used to it."

I snorted. "Excellent."

"But it did feel good to hear you call me your boyfriend." He gave me one of his killer smiles and handed me a takeout container. "Now eat something or I will get mad."

It smelled so good, and I only truly noticed then just how hungry I was. He'd bought us each a gyros snack pack, which was basically shaved gyros beef over fries with Greek yoghurt dressing and a mix of salad.

It was the best thing I'd ever eaten.

I was half done the first time I looked up to find him smiling at me. "You were starving."

"Mm," I hummed with a mouth full of food. "So good."

He laughed and stabbed some meat and fries with his fork. "So before, when I said you were on the news," he said. "I do mean on every local channel. And on the radio on my way to the kebab shop just now."

Ugh.

I rolled my eyes and groaned. "It's embarrassing. Though I've since mastered the 'I'm unavailable for comment at this time. Please stay tuned to the bureau's weather channel for updates' spiel. I didn't really think how official my comment would be. I'm not used to managing press releases."

His eyes softened. "You did great. You didn't mince your words at all."

I grimaced. "Was I too blunt? My forthrightness tends to land me in hot water." I shrugged. "But I don't see the point in sugar-coating anything, especially when talking about the severity of the storm that's coming. I know it's not my place to issue warnings in regard to evacuations and such, but she asked me what the residents of Darwin can expect. Rightfully, they should expect to evacuate."

Then I looked at him.

Oh.

"You should leave," I added with a lump of dread quickly solidifying in my belly. "You and your family. Do what you need to do with your shipping—"

"I'm not leaving."

"Tully, it's a reasonable response. There's no reason why you should stay behind. If you have the opportunity and the means to leave, you should."

His brown eyes met mine, curious and a little hurt. "Are you leaving?" he asked.

"No, I can't," I replied, gesturing to the control panels. "I have to stay."

"Then so do I." His eyes met mine, scrutinising and unblinking. "And I do have a reason to stay."

"Take your family with you—"

"Not my family, Jeremiah," he said brusquely. "You."

"I'm not worth it—"

"I beg your fuckin' pardon?!"

That stopped me so hard, I recoiled. "Pardon?"

"Don't sit there and tell me you're not worth it. Worth what, Jeremiah? What aren't you worth, exactly? What is your life not worth?"

Oh, wow.

He was actually mad at me.

"I didn't mean it like that," I mumbled, now looking at my half-eaten dinner, having lost all appetite. "I just meant . . ."

He put his container on the control panel desk, then took mine and put it there too. He took my hands and wheeled us so that our knees were touching. "Jeremiah, look at me."

My eyes met his, and where I'd expected to see anger, there was only sadness. "I'm sorry," I murmured quickly.

"You are worth staying for."

His eyes were full of sincerity. It was a little difficult for me to understand that he would want to stay for me.

"What I meant was that if you stay for me, if you stay behind *because of* me, and if something were to happen to you, I'd never forgive myself. Never."

He pulled my chair a little closer. "Then we need to make sure nothing happens to either of us."

"It's easy to say that, but Tully, this storm could be bad. And I mean *bad*."

He smirked. "I know. I watched your interview."

I rolled my eyes. "I mean it. I would be worried for you and your family. I've never been through a cyclone before. I know theoretically what to expect, but first-hand . . ." I shook my head.

"My parents have a cyclone-proof cellar, so they'll be fine. They'll take everyone in, including the old couple next door. They'll all be fine," he said. "I'll be here with you."

I stared at him. "No you won't." I looked around at the room. "Tully, this place is old, and god knows how it'll hold up."

"So why is it safe enough for you but not for me?"

"Because . . . well . . ." Damn. "That's not my point."

He laughed. "And you're forgetting one thing."

"What's that?"

"Storms are my thing. I love them."

"Yes, storms, Tully. Not cyclones."

"But I get to be here at ground zero with all the latest techn—" He glanced at the prehistoric radars. "Well, with all of last century's latest technology."

"My point exactly. It's crazy to expect you to be here."

"But I get to be here with you." His gaze met mine, all humour gone. "And maybe I am crazy. I know it sounds like it because we've known each other for just a few weeks, but, Jeremiah," he tapped my chest, "you're my kind of crazy."

His words made my heart knock against my ribs. His words, the way he looked at me, the way he always had to touch me. It made me shake my head. "I don't get it."

"Don't get what?"

"I see you and the way you look at me. I'm not stupid. I know you like me. I can see that." I ran my hand through my hair, embarrassed.

He snorted. "Yeah, of course. You're my boyfriend. I'm supposed to like you."

"But I don't get why," I whispered. "I'm waiting for the punchline or something. I don't know. I'm usually the butt of the jokes, and you're gorgeous and rich. You could have literally anyone you wanted."

He frowned at me, and from the hurt in his eyes, I knew I'd offended him. "Tully, I—"

"You know what," he said. "This is new to me too. This whole being in a relationship thing, having a boyfriend, it's all new to me. I ain't ever done this before and I feel so in over my head. I want to spend every second with you. I wanna touch you and kiss you all the fuckin' time. It gives me butterflies." He shook his head. "But if you don't feel the same . . . if I came on too strong or if you felt pressured because you got lumped here—"

I fisted his shirt, pulled him in, and kissed him, but when we broke apart, he still wouldn't look at me. God, I was going to have to say this stuff out loud. "You give me butterflies too," I whispered. "I don't know what I feel because I've never felt this before. The way you look at me, the way you hold me, it scares me because I've never . . ." I put my forehead to his chin. "It's all new to me too. But if you feel this—" I took his hand and placed it over my heart. "—then I feel the same as you."

His eyes met mine, an ocean of umber and honey. He leaned in and slowly pressed his lips to mine. "Thank you." He smiled so serenely. "I needed to hear that. And you think you can't be all mushy and shit. Look at you just now. Extra mush."

"I wasn't kidding about feeling my heart," I mumbled. "I actually feel lightheaded after saying that."

He laughed and a loud knock at the door startled us both. "I gave my key back, ya know," Doreen yelled.

I scrambled to let her in. "I'm so sorry. I didn't see you come in on the security camera."

She barged in with Bruce under one arm. "You two weren't testing the structural integrity of the control panel, were ya? Both look a little flustered."

"Uh, no," I began.

"I wanted to," Tully said cheerfully, "but he shot me down."

I was going to object, but she wasn't paying me any attention. She looked him up and down. "Jeez. You scrub up okay, doncha? Wouldn't have recognised ya if it weren't for your flash car out the front."

He grinned. "Love your shirt."

Her shirt tonight had three big Scrabble tiles across the front. *V*, *A*, and *G*.

Because of course it did. It was better than *pussy licker*, though.

Doreen laughed. "Thought I better wear a nice one in case anyone wants to interview me." Then she looked at me. "Not like Mr Significant Weather Event celebrity here."

I groaned. "Ugh. Don't remind me."

"It's the new catch phrase, apparently," Doreen said. She took her seat at the control panel. "Lock the gate on yer way out."

Okay then. That was our cue to leave.

I gave Doreen back her keys, we collected our half-eaten dinner, and Tully followed me home. I wasn't sure if we'd be continuing our conversation from before or if we'd said all that needed saying up to this point.

But he really did like me. He got butterflies because of me. As I did because of him. When he smiled at me, when he put his arms around me, when he kissed me.

It was a powerful feeling, knowing someone liked me. That *he* liked me. That this incredible man—who was miles out of my league—felt the same way about me. I wasn't kidding when I said he could have anyone . . . but for some reason he chose me.

Walking into his house, he turned the TV on, then took two beers out of the fridge and handed me one. He nodded to the balcony.

He slipped his fingers through mine and led me outside. There was a storm on the horizon. I'd been watching the radars all day, so I knew it would be brief, but there was lightning activity over the ocean.

"Ah, perfect timing," he said.

We stood there, his arm around me, his chin on my shoulder, sipping our beers, and we watched as the intracloud light show lit up the skies above, as the wind whipped around us, the smell of rain filled the air. But when some negative charge bolts hit the ocean closer to us, he pulled me inside. "I'm not risking you today, sorry," he said.

A furious downpour of rain battered the balcony the second he closed the door behind us. "Ooh, that was close," he said with a laugh.

But then his eyes cut to the television behind me. "Look, it's you!"

I turned, and sure enough, there I was on some daily news update show, where the hosts talked about daily current affairs. I understood the cyclone was an important news update, and I was interested to hear what they said after my segment.

Did they take me seriously?

Had people started evacuation plans? Were they heading south already?

I sure hoped so. I wanted them to talk about it. I

wanted them to push the importance of listening to emergency services and to evacuate if possible.

I took a swig of my beer and waited to see what they discussed.

"All seriousness aside, and we will get to the crux of the report in a moment," one host said. "How blue are his eyes?"

"I know!" the other host said, almost coming out of her seat. "Like sooo blue."

"Freakishly blue."

Jesus fucking Christ.

My heart sank, and shame washed over me.

Tully turned the TV off, tossing the remote onto the couch and pulling me against the kitchen counter. He took my beer and sat them both on the sink, then cupped his hands to my face, his nose touching mine.

"I'm sorry," he murmured. "It's just a stupid talk show. Don't pay any attention to them. They don't know what they're talking about."

"I've heard it all my life," I mumbled. "I'm used to it. I should get contacts. Brown, like yours."

"No, baby," he whispered. "I love your eyes. They're beautiful, and they're part of you. People can fuck right off. You don't change a single thing, 'kay?"

I couldn't look at him. "I'll never be taken seriously. Not ever. I deliberately didn't give my full name, because you know what comes next." I pressed my forehead to his chest, to his neck. "I'm sure all the guys at my old job think it's hilarious."

Tully wrapped his arms around me, holding me tight, so tight it was a little hard to breathe.

It felt so good.

"Fuck them," he said. "Fuck all of them. When they come knockin' next time for information or updates, tell them to fuck off."

"I already stopped taking calls," I mumbled into his neck. "I just want to do my job."

He somehow held me tighter, and we stayed like that in his kitchen for a long while, just holding each other in the dark while the storm raged on outside. Rain pelted the windows, lightning strobed the room, flashes of light in the dark.

So very fitting.

He kept our hips flush but pulled back so he could see my face. He traced his finger down my cheekbone, then thumbed my bottom lip. "You're perfect," he whispered before he kissed me.

Soft and deep. God, the way he kissed me . . . perfect, plump lips and a tangle of tongues, he showed me what perhaps he thought his words couldn't convey.

He kissed me like maybe he loved me.

Then taking my hand, he took me to bed.

CHAPTER FIVE
TULLY

I woke up when Jeremiah slipped out of bed. The sun was comin' through the windows because I'd forgotten to close the blinds last night.

God, last night.

It'd sure been something . . .

I was gonna need more gold star stickers.

While Jeremiah showered, I made coffee and toast, so at least I knew he'd eat something before he got busy all day and forgot to eat again.

He came down the stairs, dressed for work, his hair wet and smellin' all kinds of lovely. "What are you doing up?"

I handed him a cup of coffee and pushed the plate of toast toward him. "For you."

He seemed genuinely perplexed, like he did whenever I did anything nice for him. "Oh. Did you get out of bed to do this for me?"

I nodded and bit into my toast. "I was going to suggest a repeat of what we did last night but didn't want you to be late to relieve Doreen. Breakfast was option number two."

He smiled as he sipped his coffee. "Yeah, I'd rather face a nest of news reporters than an irate Doreen."

I was hopin' he'd forgotten about that. "A nest, huh? Like vipers."

"Similar." He took his toast, kissed my cheek, then my temple. "Thank you for breakfast."

"Thank you for last night."

He blushed and tried to laugh it off. "You take half the credit."

"I do regret that we didn't try out the chest monitor."

His lips twisted in a thoughtful pout. "Maybe we could try it tonight. You know, purely for scientific purposes."

I grinned at him. "That's my kind of science."

He smiled as he got to the door and stopped. "You should probably wear another gold star on your shirt today."

I laughed, surprised that he'd even mention it. "Oh I will. You should wear one too. Want me to run upstairs to get you one?"

"No, it's fine."

"I'm makin' a mental note to leave an emergency sheet of gold stickers downstairs."

He smiled. "Have a good day."

"I'm already havin' a great day."

He blushed again and ducked his head as he left, and with a happy sigh, I took my coffee and went out to the balcony. It was hard to imagine, lookin' out at the peaceful ocean to the north and the clear skies, that a massive storm was on its way.

It was hard to imagine that I was standing out there wearing nothing but boxers, smilin' at the sunrise.

I'd never been this happy.

I'd never been in love before.

And that's what this was. Stupid, far too soon, but love all the same. I'd fallen headfirst, with my whole heart, for Jeremiah.

And maybe it was too soon to admit such things. I'd already told him I liked him, that he made me feel all swoopy inside, and it made me happy to be with him.

He said he felt the same, pressing my hand above his heart. He'd finally admitted he had feelings for me, and it just did something to me.

It solidified something that I already knew.

I was so in love with him.

Not even just a little bit, but the whole way, in over my head, smiley-giddy-stupid love.

And I didn't care who knew or what anyone else thought.

I noticed my neighbour, old prudy Mrs Caddel, on her balcony in her expensive robe givin' me a scowl of disdain. Oh yes, how dare I stand on my own balcony in boxer shorts? She was lucky I was wearing anything at all.

I lifted my coffee in her direction. "Morning!"

She gave a curt nod and disappeared inside, and I snorted. I hoped she could see the scrape along my ribs to my nipple, the half hickey, half toothmark, where Jeremiah had latched onto me as he came.

A battle wound of the very best kind.

Aaaand my mind was back to everything he'd done to me last night.

Christ.

I downed my coffee and took a long, very handsy shower, wishin' it was Jeremiah—imagining it was his hand and not mine—and went to work in a very good mood.

Not even Ellis' shit-stirring digs at my smile could ruin this day.

Not even Rowan and Zoe's curious disdain.

I took my coffee and decided to answer emails and return some calls before spendin' the afternoon boarding up windows. That was the plan. I'd have to probably call into the supermarket at some point, I realised.

I probably should have done that before now.

I checked my watch. It was just on half eight. Hmm, maybe Ellis needed to go too. I picked up my desk phone and buzzed his office, but as I waited for him to pick up, my mobile phone rang.

It was Ellis, and I laughed as I answered, thinkin' he must be stuck on hold with some pain-in-the-arse customer on his desk phone. But before I could speak, he said, "Cafeteria, now."

There was no joke, no smart-arse comment. Clipped and serious.

I jumped to my feet and dashed for the cafeteria where several people—including my parents and siblings—were watchin' the TV on the wall. It was only ever on some morning show bullshit that I never had time for, but what I saw stopped me cold.

"It's all over the news," Ellis said.

It was Jeremiah's interview from yesterday. Half the screen was his face frozen, his blue eyes unmistakable. Then the other half of the screen played the very familiar footage of his mother on Collins Street, the tramline being struck by lightning, her doing that macabre dance, his stroller rolling away. Then it showed a policeman carrying a crying toddler, a small boy with dark hair and very, very blue eyes.

The screen froze, Jeremiah's face on both sides of the screen. From yesterday and from all those years ago.

Jesus fucking Christ.

What he'd said last night came back to me.

I never said my full name because you know what comes next.

He was exactly right. He knew. He *knew* this would happen.

"Those motherfuckers," I said, feeling a rage explode within me. An anger like I'd never known.

"Is that really him?" Ellis asked. "Was that his mother?"

I managed to look at him, at all the faces now watching me. And despite how angry I was, I was hurt for Jeremiah so much more. This was going to kill him. "Yes, that's him. I need to go."

I turned and ran, only stopping to grab my keys and phone from my desk, and I raced to my car.

Fuck all those arseholes.

Christ.

When Jeremiah had said he has to relive his mother dying every time that footage was played, I never really understood . . .

Until *now*.

How dare they.

How fucking dare they.

I sped the whole way to his work. I was way past caring. And of course there were news vans parked at the gate, which was, thankfully, locked.

At least they weren't banging on his door.

I skidded the Rover to a stop, maybe a little too close to them, gaining the attention of every reporter and camera there. I got out and slammed my door, getting madder by the damn second.

They weren't here for emergency news updates. They were here for nothin' but gossip.

"You wanna be careful," one cameraman said, nodding his chin to my car.

I spun and pointed my finger at him. "And you might wanna watch your fuckin' mouth."

No, *now* I had their complete and undivided attention.

"You all come here for what?" I asked. "This office is trying to do a job, obtaining information that will save lives, and you're all here for fuckin' what? You wanna broadcast footage of a mother dying in front of her kid, for ratings, then expect him to, what? Come out for an interview? Every single one of you can fuck right off. You want news? Go back to your offices and wait for official bulletin releases. Or do what they suggested yesterday and leave Darwin—and just keep fucking drivin'."

I noticed a few of them look behind me, into the yard, their eyes widening. And when I glanced back, I saw why.

Doreen was coming across the yard, whistling a cheerful tune, and swingin' her baseball bat, just as two police cruisers arrived. "Right on time," Doreen said as she walked up, still swingin' her bat. "If any of you leeches had a fuckin' brain cell between ya's, you'd know blocking access to a government building is a *big* no-no."

The cops got out, and while they began to speak to the reporters, asking them to move along, Doreen opened the gate for me.

The reporters and cameramen slowly dispersed, but not before giving me a lengthy glare and getting in their vehicles.

"Thanks, Hewy," Doreeen said.

One of the cops, the oldest of them, gave her a nod. "No worries, Dori. You weren't actually gonna use that bat, were ya?"

"Nah." She winked. "Nice day for a home run, doncha reckon?"

He grinned and went back to the remaining reporters, and I looked up at Doreen. "How is he?"

She shrugged her reply, meaning not great.

So I ran across the yard and up the stairs. I pulled open the door and found him at the control panel. He'd surely been watching the security screen and seen it all.

And all the anger I'd felt, that rage that had fuelled me, melted away.

"Hey," I said gently.

His eyes met mine.

"You okay?"

"I'm fine."

No, he wasn't.

I went over and spun his chair so I could kneel in front of him. "Jeremiah, baby, it's okay to not be okay."

He sagged and gave the slightest shake of his head. "I knew it would happen. It's like a shadow I won't ever be rid of."

I put my hand to his face. "I'm so sorry. I came as soon as I saw."

He closed his eyes. "Doreen went home, got a news flash on her phone, and came straight back," he murmured. "She thought it was just going to be the interview, so she watched it. She knew . . . she didn't think I should be here alone. She didn't have to come back . . ."

I knew I liked her for a reason.

"Thank god she did." With my hand at the back of his neck, I tugged him forward and all but lifted him to his feet so I could hug him properly. "I'm so fucking mad," I hissed. "I can't imagine how you feel."

"Just . . . sad."

I hugged him tighter and rubbed the back of his head. "I got you."

He nodded against my throat but didn't say anything for a few beats. "Thank you," he said, so softly. So sad. "I've never had anyone care before."

I pulled back and put my forehead to his. "I care. A whole fuckin' lot."

Doreen came through the door, stood the bat up in the small entryway, and Jeremiah immediately stepped away from me. I didn't care what Doreen thought, and I knew for a fact she wouldn't care. I kept my hand on his back so he'd know I wasn't going anywhere.

"Well, me and Bruce'll be off now," she said.

I hadn't even noticed the dog.

"Stay with him," she said to me, nodding to Jeremiah.

"I plan to. Thank you for coming back."

I also only just noticed that her fresh shirt had *read my lips* written on it with a somewhat artistic image of a vulva on it. Yeah, there was no way they were showing any footage of that on the news. Not without a lot of pixelating.

"Gonna grab some shuteye. I'll lock the gate on my way out, and I'll be back at eight tonight." She scooped up Bruce. "And Tully, I heard what you said to those leeches out the front. Good for you. If they come back, don't be scared to swing that bat around."

Oh. Yeah, I probably wouldn't do that. But then I remembered how angry I'd been. Maybe I would . . .

Then, on her way out, she peered closer to the radar. "Yeah, he ain't slowin' down any. If you're stickin' around, how about boardin' the place up a bit? There's some pieces cut to size from last time."

I nodded. "Sure. I'll be here."

"Good lad."

And with that, she was gone.

Jeremiah all but fell into his chair. "You don't have to stay," he mumbled.

I lifted his chin and leaned down to peck his lips. "I'm not leaving."

I pulled over Bruce's chair and parked my arse in it, then studied the radar screen and in particular the very large, somewhat circular cloud band moving in our direction. "Sooo," I said brightly. "This doesn't look good."

Jeremiah almost smiled. "Yeah. As Doreen said, it's not slowing down any. In fact, it's just gathering steam."

"Still on track for here?"

He nodded. "Dead on."

One of the other screens started to beep and he had to switch something over to something else and relay some data stream to another office, and for a guy who'd never seen a dash as old as this just a short while ago, he was all over it now.

"I should look and see what I can board your windows up with," I said, gettin' up. I went to move past him to the far end where all the ancient field equipment was—I was sure I'd seen planks of plyboard there at some point—and he grabbed my hand.

"Thank you," he murmured. "I didn't mean to sound ungrateful before."

I squeezed his hand. "You didn't."

He sighed. "I should probably call my dad."

My heart sank for him. "Okay. Want me to sit with you while you speak to him?"

He did smile then, somewhat sad but laced with gratitude. "No, it's fine."

"I'll be here, just showing off my handyman skills." I gently lifted his chin and kissed him. "I'm not leaving."

He nodded, a little happier now. "Thank you."

I left him to it. Albeit I couldn't go far; the office was tiny and there really wasn't anywhere *to* go. And the windows that needed boarding up were small. One in the toilet room and one long narrow one under the eaves. The office was basically a dark cave. But I found the plyboard Doreen had mentioned and a drill that was so old it needed to be plugged into a power outlet.

There was a steel ladder fixed to the back of the building, which was incredibly helpful, given all the aerials and satellites on the small roof area, though it was so hot in the Darwin sun, it almost seared straight through my hand when I grabbed it.

I went back in, grabbed Jeremiah's keys and moved the Jeep over, and stood on the hood instead.

He had his phone pressed to his ear when I went in, though he wasn't talking. I could hear the mumble of his father's voice, and Jeremiah was frowning.

I hated that he had to live with this.

It wasn't his fault. He'd done nothin' wrong. In fact, he'd done the *right* thing by issuing a statement when asked of the dangers of the coming storm when that reporter had asked.

I guess he'd learned a lesson though, as the new boss of the Darwin office. To never give those arseholes anything. Issue all statements via bulletins and offer no interviews, ever. And if any of 'em ever needed anything—anything at all—it'd be a flat fucking no.

It took me a while to get the boards in place and fixed to the window frames. Doreen wasn't kidding when she said she thought the boards were the ones used last time. I wasn't sure when the last time was, but they were old and this would be their last use.

Everything at this office was outdated, like they'd been forgotten when every other Bureau of Meteorology office probably had state of the art gear.

I had to wonder how that made Jeremiah feel.

Had they shoved him in this post so he'd be forgotten too?

Probably.

I hated them all.

I went back in, determined to try and brighten his day. Before I could ask him how the phone call with his father went, he nodded to my phone where I'd left it on the console.

"Your phone buzzed a lot," he said.

I gave his shoulder a squeeze. "How was your dad?" I sat down and picked up my phone.

His only reply was a shrug.

I had three missed calls from Ellis and a text message.

> Ah bro, you're in the shit now. Call back.

Then a few minutes after that, I had two missed calls from my father and one text. And he *never* texted.

You need to call me. Now.

Shit.

"Well, this isn't good," I mumbled, showing Jeremiah the text, and hit Call. "Dad," I said. "It's me."

He sighed. Not a relieved sigh, but a disappointed one. "I take it you've seen the news?"

"Yeah, I did. That's why I came to see Jeremiah. I was with you in the cafeteria—"

"Not that news. The latest news."

Cold prickled at my scalp. "No. Why, what happened?"

"Just you, ranting and swearing at the news reporters at the bureau office?"

"That was on the news?" I didn't remember any of them filming.

"Yes, it was on the news," Dad hissed at me. "There was a lot of words beeped out, which I should probably be grateful for."

I made a disgusted sound. "You know what? Fuck them. They deserved everything I said, and I'm not sorry."

"You should be sorry!" he said, a little too loudly. It reminded me of when he'd get mad at us kids for doing something stupid. He hadn't yelled at me like that in years. *Shit, he is really mad.* "Tully, do me a favour and look down at the shirt you're wearing. And tell me what the *hell you were thinking!*"

I looked down at my shirt . . . at my work shirt, with our company logo across my left pec.

Oh no.

"Oh shit," I mumbled, covering it with my hand—what good it did now was anyone's guess. "Oh fu . . . Dad, I'm sorry. I didn't realise. I didn't think. I was just so freakin' mad at what they'd done, and then when I saw them all lined up at the gate like wolves at the door." My eyes met Jeremiah's. "I'll issue an apology on behalf of the company, or—"

"You'll do no such thing," my father said. He was definitely in boss mode now. "You'll not say another word. I don't care if they shove a camera in your face, you will keep your head down. Say no comment, or better yet, say nothing at all."

Hmm.

Yeah, I don't think so.

Anger flared in my belly, burning hot in my chest.

"You know what, Dad?" I said. "I fucked up and I'm sorry for that. But if those leeches come for Jeremiah again, I won't keep my head down, and I won't keep my mouth shut."

Jeremiah slid his hand onto my knee and shook his head, silently telling me no.

It only solidified my resolve. "What they did was wrong, Dad," I continued. "Where's their accountability? Where's their apology to him? And I won't apologise for what I said or how I said it because for that, I'm not fuckin' sorry."

"Tully—" he snapped, but my mother's softer tone cut him off.

"Tully," she said, "for what it's worth, personally, we agree with you. But professionally, we now have a media PR circus to deal with, on top of emergency shipping offloads, fast-tracking quarantine regs, clearing the docks, and battening down hatches."

I sighed, running my hand through my hair. I felt bad enough, but gawd, a mother's disappointment weighed too damn much.

"I'm sorry," I whispered.

"What time will you be home?" she asked.

"After eight," I replied. "I'm not leaving Jeremiah here by himself."

Jeremiah frowned at me. "I'll be okay, you can go if you need," he whispered, just as another alert came through that he had to switch the alarm off for.

"Then we'll be at your place after eight," Mum said. "We'll bring dinner."

I wasn't sure what to say. What could I say? Not that it mattered, because the line went dead. I tossed my phone onto the control panel. "Fuck."

"What happened?" Jeremiah asked. "I heard most of what your father said, sorry. He spoke rather loudly."

I sighed again. "My little tirade at those fuckers at the gate this morning made the news."

"Oh."

I pointed to the company logo on my chest. "With some prime-time advertising, apparently."

His eyes widened with realisation. "Oh no."

"Yeah. Anyway, my parents will be at my place when we get there. So that's gonna be a lot of fun. I mean, it's not the arse-reaming I had in mind for tonight. My father is pissed." Not sure what else I could do, I stood up and ran both hands through my hair. "Fuck!"

Jeremiah stood up and took my hand. "Hey," he breathed. "I'm sorry. I didn't—"

"It's not your fault. I lost my cool at those reporters. I was so fuckin' mad for what they did to you. While I was wearing my father's company name on my shirt."

His brow furrowed as we studied my knuckles. "It seems a day for both of us to disappoint our fathers."

Oh god. The phone call he had with his dad . . .

I sagged and pulled him into my arms. He slid against me easily, our arms holding each other like interlocking parts.

It felt so good.

His embrace, his touch, soothing away my pain and anger, was healing me in real time. I held him tighter, not wanting to let go.

Not now, not ever.

"Was your dad okay?"

He hummed a non-committal sound. "Same as always. He said it wasn't my fault while also implying I should know better."

"I'm sorry," I murmured.

He tried to pull back, but I kept him held fast. "Mm-mm," I mumbled. I wanted to help him forget the shitty morning we'd had, so keeping my arms around him, I sat myself down slowly on the console dash, leaning against it while holding onto him. It really was the perfect height . . .

"Hmm," I hummed against his neck. "You could fuck me on this." I lifted one leg as proof.

He chuckled and managed to pull back a little. His hips were still flush to mine, so I didn't object too much.

"Maybe if we didn't have a life-threatening weather event aiming right at us."

"Ooh." I smiled. "That wasn't a no."

He gripped my other thigh and lifted it, pressing me hard against the controls. "No, it wasn't a no."

"Damn. Maybe we could see how many alarms we can set off and how many weather warnings we can issue across the Territory. We could keep a whiteboard with our different scores on it for each time."

He chuckled, and our attempt at joking our way out of our miseries seemed to have worked. Him pushing against all my best spots didn't hurt either. I didn't even mind the buttons and switches pressing into my back.

He rested his forehead on mine and gave me a soft kiss. "Thank you for being here."

I pecked his lips with a smile. "Don't thank me yet. We have to get through dinner with my folks first. If you still want to thank me after that, I'll take payment in sexual grati-*fuck*-ation."

He smirked. "I'm almost certain that's not how that word sounds."

"Pretty sure it is."

And of course, the data feed for something or other began to buzz, and after that it was a weather warning for the top east corner of the state with high precipitation forecast, and then it was an alert for cattle graziers in the bottom part of the Territory because of possible flash flooding in usually dry riverbeds.

It just never stopped. And it was for all of the Northern Territory, a land area twice the size of Texas. He had a lot to cover, and it wasn't just the monstrous cloud band swirling its way toward us that he had to work around. It was all kinds of weather.

Needless to say, it was a busy day for him.

I just got to sit there and watch him be awesome. I fed him and kept him watered, and I texted intermittently with my brother who just loved that I was the one in my parents' bad books for a change.

I was so not lookin' forward to tonight.

When Doreen arrived a bit before eight, I almost wanted to tell her that she could go home, that we'd stay instead . . . but I had to face the music, and quite frankly, Jeremiah needed some downtime. He needed some rest.

I just had to make sure he got that, and not a standoff between me and my parents.

I didn't see any reporters on my way home, and I was going to tell Jeremiah that I'd take a different route to him—because reporters couldn't follow us both— when I realised I didn't care if they saw us go home together.

In fact, I kinda hoped they would.

Yeah, clearly I was still in the pissed-off and defensive stage.

When we got to my house, it wasn't just my parents who were already there, but my two brothers' cars were there as well.

And that little seed of anger and defensiveness sprouted into a whopping tree of rage.

Was this a whole family meeting? Were they all going to stare at me and give me the 'we're so disappointed' lectures? Because I wasn't about to cop that.

I got out of my car and held Jeremiah's door for him. He saw me glaring at the offending cars, and he nodded toward them before the roller door blocked them from view. "Who else is here?" he asked.

"Ellis," I replied. "And Rowan."

"Oh." He looked uncomfortable. "Your eldest brother's here too?"

The brother I wasn't particularly close to. "Yeah. Look, Jeremiah, if you want to hang out upstairs, that's fine with me. I'll face the firing squad and—"

"I'm not leaving you," he said, a hint of determination in those incredible eyes.

I couldn't help but smile. "Come on, let's get this over with."

I took his hand and led him in through the laundry to a scene I hadn't expected.

At all.

My mum was in the kitchen. She was cooking something that smelled great, but on the balcony . . . was my dad and two brothers boarding up the glass panels.

"Uh, what's going on?" I asked, surprised. Shocked, if I was being honest.

Mum looked up from the dishes of food and gave us a smile. "We figured you'd been so busy you wouldn't have had time to take care of your house. I used your spare key." She walked over, took Jeremiah's arm, and led him into the kitchen. "Tully, go help your brothers. And behave yourself. There's a drill and a nail gun involved, and quite frankly, I don't want to explain any intentional mishaps to the ER doctors."

Intentional mishaps.

I snorted, still shocked, and seeing Mum enlist Jeremiah into her duty list, I went out onto the balcony.

"Oh, look who it is," Ellis said. "Blister's here. Always shows up after the hard work is done."

"Ellis, hold it straight," Rowan grumbled.

"I am holding it straight," Ellis griped.

Rowan drilled the screw in, then stood back to look at the slightly crooked board. He tried to whack Ellis with the drill. "Shoulda went to Specsavers, dickhead."

"Tully, hold this," Dad said, lifting another board into place. I held it and Dad fired a nail into it. Thank god he had the nail gun and not the other two.

"Oh look, it's the only straight thing Tully's ever done in his life," Ellis said.

I tried to take the nail gun from Dad but he wouldn't give it to me. "For Christ's sake, boys," Dad said. "Ellis and Rowan, go upstairs and start on the bedroom windows."

Ellis, who now had the drill, gave it a few whirrs. "Not the only thing getting drilled in there, huh, Tull?"

I wrestled the nail gun off Dad, but by the time I got my hands on it, Ellis had already laughed his dumb arse up the stairs.

I considered going up after him but thought better of it. With a sigh, I gave it back to Dad. "I could make it look like an accident."

He rolled his eyes. "Get the next board."

I held the plyboard in place, realising that now Dad and I were alone, it was probably a good time to talk.

"Look," I started. "About today. I'm sorry I dragged the business into it. I'm sorry for the shitstorm I created.

It negatively impacts you and Mum, and everyone, I guess. I just didn't think. I saw them and I was so freakin' pissed off, I wanted to strangle them. I didn't even think about the shirt I was wearing."

He nailed the board into place. "What's done is done. I accept your apology, and I do understand. Your mother explained it to me, and I get it. At first I was mad because it was reckless and unprofessional, but she told me what was really going on, and she asked me what I'd do if the media treated her like that, and I get it. Yes, it created a media stir, but it's nothing we can't handle. We have a legal team—"

"I'm sorry," I said. But I was also confused. "Mum explained what to you? What's really going on?"

Dad fired another nail into the next corner of the board and looked at me. "That you love him. You were protecting someone you love."

The world tilted a little and blood pounded in my ears.

What?

"Pardon?"

"I mean, we were all kinda shocked with how you behaved with him in front of us. We ain't ever seen you be like that with anyone, all cute and smiling, touchy-feely and whatever." His cheeks ran pink. "I guess I just thought it was . . . fun and exciting, or physical. Or whatever. But you're living together already, so . . ."

None of anything he was saying was making sense.

He studied me. "Ah jeez, Tully," he said. "Are you telling me you don't? Because your mother is a good gauge at these things. You know she said that Rowan would marry Diah from the second he saw her because of some look in his eyes. I dunno, I didn't see it. But she did. Same with Zoe. Said her and Chris'd be married within the year because of the way Zoe looked at him. Guess she saw it in you and the way you look at him. I dunno how these things work, but she hasn't been wrong yet."

I tried to swallow.

"How . . . how did I look at him?"

Dad sighed and gave my shoulder a squeeze. "Are you saying you don't have feelings for him?"

"Yeah, of course I do," I whispered. "I . . . I love him. I haven't told him that yet though, and I didn't expect to hear it from you. But I've never felt like this about anyone. He's . . . he's amazing, and I want to be with him all the time. The idea of not being with him makes me feel sick. I could spend every minute of every day with him and it's still not enough. I . . . want to do everything I can to make him happy."

Dad smiled at me, a little proud, a little teary. "Sounds like love to me."

CHAPTER SIX

JEREMIAH

Dinner with Tully's parents and his two brothers was not what I'd been expecting.

I'd been expecting them to rebuke him for the public tirade whilst wearing a company shirt thing. I had been expecting that because Tully had been.

Especially from his father and perhaps Rowan.

But it never came.

Instead, they boarded up all the glass doors and windows while his mother got dinner ready. She made me help, with which I was no help at all, I'm sure. But while we busied ourselves in the kitchen, she asked me about the office and the new job, and if I was happy to have left Melbourne.

She asked me how I was finding Darwin and the terrible heat. She asked me if I actually enjoyed my time at the bunker in the middle of Kakadu or if I was just saying that to make Tully happy.

She was horrified and somewhat dismayed when I told her I'd loved it. That I couldn't wait to go again.

She'd sighed dramatically, and said it was no wonder Tully was so smitten with me.

I certainly hadn't been expecting that.

We ate dinner at the dining table, and while it was an informal dinner, I did feel a little scrutinised. Especially by Rowan. He was polite, of course, but he was also curious and asked me about my doctorate and dissertation, and even though it was general conversation, it somehow felt as if I was being interviewed.

To see if I was good enough for his brother.

Ellis had grinned, about to speak, until Tully—while making direct eye contact with Ellis—took the carving knife from the tray of roast chicken and put it beside his plate. A silent threat, but Ellis wisely chose not to make any jokes at our expense.

I didn't have any siblings, or a close family for that matter, so I never had this . . . feeling. Sure, there was antagonism and snarkiness between them, but it was clear they all loved each other very much.

I envied them.

I envied them a great deal.

Though something else I noticed over the course of the evening was Tully's behaviour toward me.

He sat with his hand on my thigh for most of dinner and I caught him looking at me, as if he was trying to figure out a complex equation in his head.

He was still very much himself, but something was different.

Maybe it was just that Rowan and Ellis were sitting opposite us, or that his parents were at either end of the table.

They never mentioned the media circus. Not to me, anyway. But I suspected his father had said something on the matter when they were fixing the glass panels on the balcony.

I was still grateful.

Then his father asked me when to expect Hazer's pre-show. He'd been a boy during Cyclone Tracy, apparently. "I remember it all too well," he said.

"As early as tomorrow evening," I said. "The frontal system will bring the beginning of the storm. Rain, wind gusts, sea swells, as I'm sure with which you're familiar. Hazer will likely be a two-day event, from the first rainfall, beginning to end. The cyclone is expected to touch down at 7:00 am the day after tomorrow. It's difficult to predict its behavioural pattern once it crosses land, but we can make educated projections." They all stared at me, and I tried to lighten the mood. "It's not too late to leave. You'd only have to drive a hundred kilometres south, maybe two. I estimate Hazer will progress east once it hits land. The change of atmospheric pressure will cause the storm front to ride the warmer ocean winds, so effectively it will mow through the coastline toward the Gulf of Carpentaria. It should downgrade in intensity once it hits though, but if you do decide to leave, please take Tully with you. By force if necessary." I looked at Tully and grimaced. I never should have opened my mouth. "I don't believe it's deemed kidnapping if it endeavours to save your life."

Tully chuckled, his eyes warm, and his fingers slid over mine. On the table, in front of them all. "I'm not leaving you," he said simply. "I told you that. And I'm pretty sure kidnapping is still kidnapping."

I noticed Rowan's eyes draw down to our joined hands, and when he glanced up, his focus was solely on Tully. A fond smile softened his features for a moment until Ellis nudged his elbow. "Told ya. He's a goner."

Tully shot him a glare and Mr Larson quickly grabbed the carving knife out of Tully's reach. "So, Jeremiah," Mr Larson said. "Hazer. What kind of name is that?"

"It's an Arabic name, common in Malaysia and Indonesia," I explained. "It means to be prepared, be ready."

They were all staring at me again. "Well, if that's not an omen," Rowan said glumly. Then he sighed. "I should get going. I left Diah to do dinner and put the kids to bed."

"I appreciate you being here," Tully said. "Is your house boarded up?"

He nodded. "Yeah."

"I'll get Jeremiah to work tomorrow and come around to help whoever needs it," he said.

I wanted to argue that I didn't need him to escort me but thought that might be a conversation best left for when we were alone. And the truth was, I really had needed him today . . .

"We should all be going," Mrs Larson said. "Ellis, help me clean this—"

"Please leave it. I'll take care of it," I offered. "It's the least I can do."

She grimaced, as if she wanted to argue but didn't

want to offend, and Tully laughed. "Mum, don't argue with him. He's feisty, and he knows really big words."

I levelled a glare at him but it waned with the smile he aimed right at me.

"Gawd," Ellis drawled as he stood up. "Someone save me. The sappiness is killing me."

"Eat shit, nut sac," Tully said.

"Boys," their mother chided. She stood and we all got to our feet as well; then they made their way to the door.

When they were leaving, his mother had given Tully a kiss on the cheek and led him toward their car for a private conversation, I deduced. So, giving them some privacy, I went back inside and began cleaning up dinner.

I was washing up the few things that wouldn't fit in the dishwasher when he came back in. "Everything okay?" I asked.

He leaned against the kitchen counter, took a tea towel, and began drying a tray. "Yeah, yeah." He nodded. "I apologise for Ellis. He's a pain in my arse."

"Your brothers are great. Both of them. I wasn't sure what to expect of Rowan—I think you made him out to be this big bad guy—but he's very nice. He cares for you a great deal."

Tully seemed to mull that over before he nodded. "I know."

"I think he bears the responsibility of being the eldest child, the one on whose shoulders the company falls."

"I know. I never meant to give you the impression

he was a bad guy, sorry." Tully put the tray down and picked up the next. "I was expecting them to rip me a new arsehole when I saw their cars here." He let out a sigh. "Guess maybe that was me knowing I would have deserved it."

"They didn't come to rip you a new one," I said gently. "They came to support you. To rally around you because you'd made a mistake. That just proves what an amazing family you have."

His eyes met mine. "I apologised to my father, and he said . . . some stuff."

"What kind of stuff?"

He looked down at the tray he was holding, and his cheeks tinted pink. "Just . . . stuff I didn't think I was ready to hear from him but I dunno, maybe I am."

"Like what?" I rinsed the bubbles off my hands and dried them on the tea towel he was holding. "About me?"

His eyes cut to mine. "What? Did my mother say something to you?"

So definitely about me then . . .

"Do they not like me?" I suddenly felt a little unwell. "I tried to stop talking at the end there, about the cyclone and maybe kidnapping you, but I was nervous because they were all looking at me—"

"What? No," he said with a laugh, taking my hand. "The opposite, actually. My mum thinks you're great."

"Oh." My stomach was on a seesaw. "Then what is it?"

He looked at our hands, his thumb sweeping nervously across my knuckles, and he smiled and shook his head. He whispered, "I don't know . . . I don't know if I'm ready to say just yet."

Outside, thunder rumbled and a crack of lightning echoed through the sky from a few kilometres away.

We both turned to the balcony, but the glass doors were all boarded up. "This place looks like a prison cell," he mumbled. Taking my hand, he pressed my palm to his lips and his eyes met mine, a different depth to them now. "Take me to bed, Jeremiah. Have your way with me. I want you inside me while the storm rages outside."

Oh.

Well, then.

I lifted his chin and kissed him softly. "Are you sure? After last night—"

Something fierce flickered in his eyes, and there was no doubt.

He was sure.

Still holding his hand, I led him toward the stairs. He hit the light switch on the way, and his room, with the windows all covered with plyboard, was pitch-black. I went to turn the lights on, but he grabbed my arm and pulled me close.

"Go by feel," he murmured.

Oh boy.

My body already on edge, I did what he wanted. I raked my hands up his chest, feeling along his neck so I could undo the top buttons on his polo shirt. I pulled it over his head, quickly cupping his jaw so I could line up a kiss.

I teased his tongue with mine, pulling him in close

and skimming my hands down his back and over his arse and back up again. My hands explored and mapped out every inch while I sucked on his tongue.

He fumbled with the button on his pants, and I gripped his hands to stop him. "You said I could have my way," I murmured.

He made a sound that was more groan than gasp. My eyes had adjusted to the complete darkness, enough that I could see the outline of the side of his face, his eyes, and . . .

And the way he was looking at me.

Not even the darkness could hide that.

I undid his pants and slid my hands under his briefs so I could push them down. He pulled at the buttons on my shirt and then tried for the button on my pants. I wound my fingers around his wrists and stopped him. "Get on the bed," I said.

He groaned again. "Fuck yes."

I stripped out of my clothes while he complied and had to rummage around blindly for the bedside table. "Ow," I said when I caught my finger on the edge of a foil wrapper. Tully chuckled, but it became a moan when I kneeled on the bed, finding one of his feet first and making my way up his leg.

I kissed up his thigh, getting close to his crotch. "Hmm," I hummed, inhaling his scent.

His fingers found my hair. "Don't torture me, please."

"I'm going by feel," I whispered, finding the base of his cock and nudging his balls with my nose. Then I licked a stripe up the underside of his shaft.

"Oh fuck."

Thunder boomed overhead and he pulled on my hair and arched his back. "Jeremiah," he whispered.

Pleading.

I found the lube where I'd thrown it on the bed, and spreading his legs wide, I smeared his hole and pressed a finger into him. He grunted, not a happy sound.

I stopped. "Tully?"

"I need more," he said. "Not your fingers. I need your cock inside me. I need you to fuck me, Jeremiah. No games tonight. I'm serious."

"Tully, I—"

He reached up, blindly grabbed at my face, my neck, and pulled me up to meet him. His legs wrapped around my waist. "What part of 'I need you to fuck me' didn't you understand?" He crushed his mouth to mine for a bruising kiss and rocked his hips up, searching for what he wanted.

What he needed.

With my tongue in his mouth, I lifted his left leg up, my cock sliding against his hole, and he whined. "Do it, just . . . please."

It would have been so easy to push inside him.

Condom . . .

Condom.

Jesus.

Panting, I pulled back and went to my knees. I put that condom on so damn fast I almost injured myself, and when an impatient, frustrated Tully realised what I was doing, he laughed . . .

Until I lifted his legs up to his chest and sank my cock inside him.

His eyes wide, he gasped out a cry and groaned on the exhale. He tried to arch his back but I pinned him with my hips and sank all the way in, sinking my tongue into his mouth at the same time.

He dug his fingernails into me, clawing at my back . . . until he fully surrendered. Then he pulled me closer and we found a rhythm, slow, long, and deep. He held my face, his eyes imploring, the colour of burned honey and forever.

"Jeremiah," he whispered before sucking on my bottom lip.

This was different than before. All the times we'd done this had been amazing, but this . . . this was more.

My heart was in this. Beating in time with his, joined in the most intimate of ways.

I thrust in deep, his body a glove of warmth taking me all the way in. I tried to get my arms underneath him so I could get closer, impossibly closer. He wrapped his arms around me as if he understood.

As if he felt it too.

This shift between us.

Closer, something unspoken exchanged between us. In his eyes, in the way he held me, the way he took me. I never wanted it to end. I never wanted this feeling to stop, as a storm we couldn't see raged outside. Here, in his bed, in his arms, this was euphoria, this was ecstasy.

This was making love.

I crushed my mouth to his, our tongues tangled, and when I tasted his tears, I pulled back. His eyes were wet and glassy. I cupped his face, my forehead to his, and I stopped thrusting, holding as still as I could. "Are you okay?"

He nodded quickly. "Please don't stop. God, Jeremiah, please."

I pulled out to the tip and pushed all the way back in, and he groaned my name, over and over. His eyes rolled back in his head, he pushed his head back, his neck corded, and his whole body went rigid in my arms. His cock, untouched and swollen, jerked and he cried out as his warmth spilled between us.

When his arms fell away and all resistance was gone, he gave me his body. I drove into him again and again, as deep as I could, until I couldn't hold back anymore. I came so hard, with my whole body, with my whole heart.

And when I came back to my senses, when the room stopped spinning, he was tracing circles on my back, kissing my neck, my collarbone, my shoulder.

I pulled out of him but rolled us onto our sides, quickly wrapping him up in my arms. "Are you okay?"

He nodded into the crook of my neck. "Was intense, that's all."

I lifted his chin and kissed him softly. "It was. Glad you felt the same."

His eyes scanned mine, the room still dark but we'd adjusted to it now, enough to see his face close up, anyway. "You felt it too? Do you . . . feel the same?"

My heart rate kicked back up a gear. Okay wow, we were going to discuss this . . . "I feel . . . something I've never felt before," I said, laying my truth bare. "I'm not sure . . . I, uh . . . God."

He snorted out a laugh, his hand to my cheek. "I said somethin' similar to my dad tonight."

Wait, what?

"Uh, you did what?"

Tully sighed, his sleepy eyes heavy-lidded and dreamy. "My dad, he said somethin' to me tonight. Somethin' I didn't think I was ready to talk about, but who knows, maybe I am."

I brushed his long blond hair from his forehead. "And what's that?"

"I'm falling in love with you," he whispered. "But I've never . . . I mean, I know what love is, but what I feel for you is so much more. I dunno how to explain it. And I don't expect you to say anything back. That's not why I told you. Ellis thinks I'm a hopeless sap because none of my family have ever seen me be with anyone else the way I am with you. God, this is embarrassing." He laughed and tried to duck his face, but I made him look at me.

I planted a soft kiss on his lips. "Tully—"

"It's okay," he blurted. "I don't expect you to say anything. I just wanted you to know, because . . . well, I don't know why. Because you deserve to be loved. God, I fell so hard, so fast, it's crazy, but you . . . you're someone very special to me, Jeremiah. And if you wanna know the real reason my dad and brother didn't rip me a new arsehole, it's because my mother told them they couldn't. She said it was very obvious that I was in love with you and therefore it was off limits because she would expect my dad to do for her exactly what I did for you." He sighed. "When Dad said that—you know, the L-word—I almost died, but you know what? They're right. I do. I love you. I knew I was in love with you but just wasn't sure if I was ready to hear it." He traced his finger from my temple to my cheek. "Pretty sure I fell for you back at the bunker when you went out into the storm and almost got hit by lightning and you raced back and slid under the side wall like an action-movie star. Pretty sure my heart saw that and went, 'Yep, you know what? That's a done deal right there. That's your person, Tully.' And honestly, the pissing into the empty bottle and givin' it to the crocodiles to drink was just an added bonus."

I burst out laughing. "I didn't give it to the crocodiles to drink."

He chuckled, his eyes searching mine. Happy, serene.

In love.

I traced my thumb along his bottom lip, my heart two sizes too large for my chest, knocking against my ribs, urging me to say something . . .

"I feel it too," I whispered. "To be honest, it scares me because . . . well, because I don't know what love is. I have no experience in talking about emotions. Growing up with my dad, he was very closed off. I threw myself into my studies, and my only experience with men involved brief encounters—"

"In bathroom stalls."

"Exactly." I managed an embarrassed smile. "But I think it's . . . what you said. When I look at you . . . God,

Tully, I can't talk about this because I've never talked about this stuff." I closed my eyes and laughed. "My god, you should feel my heart."

He laughed and put his palm to my chest. "Oh, where's your watch?"

"I took it off. It would have melted on my wrist if it measured what we just did."

He laughed, his eyes bright, his smile wide. "Such a shame. I'd have loved for it to send out a health distress alert to the ambos. We could have given them a show."

I chuckled. "I'm sure paramedics have seen worse."

"Worse? God, they'd be strapped to see better, I can tell you that much. Christ, that was hot. Possibly the best sex of my life. You made me cry, and that's a first."

I kissed him. "Because it wasn't just sex."

His smile faded into something more serene, his eyes intense. "No, it wasn't."

"So are you just going to ignore the fact that I told you I felt the same?" I asked. "And how much it scares me? Is that something we're just going to gloss over? Because I've never said that to anyone in my entire life. Not even my father."

"Nothing scares you. I've seen you not even flinch when lightning hit the ground fifty metres from you."

I scanned his eyes. If only he knew how wrong he was. "You terrify me."

He breathed in deep and sighed happily. "You feel the same."

I nodded.

"But you struggle to say it because you were never shown love."

I swallowed, suddenly not feeling so blissful. "Well, yeah. I guess."

Tully cupped my face, making me look at him. "If you feel what I feel, then you feel love." I gave the smallest of nods and he smiled. "Your dad might not be able to show you he loves you or tell you, but I'm sure he loves you."

I shrugged. "We've never spoken about . . . any emotions. At all. Ever."

He kissed me. "I'm gonna show you so much love you won't know what to do with it."

"I already don't know what to do with it, to be honest."

He laughed. "Well, let's start with a shower. I need to get cleaned up because I'm sticky and lubed all over."

"Oh." I let him escape my arms, only really feeling the stickiness when he had to peel himself off me.

After almost blinding us both when I flipped the light switch on in the bathroom, I started the shower and pulled him under the spray, lathering up the sponge with shower gel and giving him a thorough washing. He had to wash his hair—not entirely sure how we got lube up there, but anyway—I made a point of taking care of him, looking after him with tender touches and soft kisses.

I might not be able to tell him with words, but I could do this for him.

He hummed and leaned into every touch, looking at me with puppy dog eyes. "You do love me," he murmured. I smiled and ducked my head, nowhere to hide under the bright lights and being completely naked. He laughed and booped me on the nose with a soapy finger. "I know you do."

I met his gaze and gave him an embarrassed, reluctant nod.

He did a little happy dance. "I will make you say it one day. You'll be able to say it as easy as talking about the weather. Which, for you, is easy-peasy." I rolled my eyes and he gave me a playful shove. "Now get out," he said. "I need to soak under this water jet a little longer. Unless you'd like to give me round two in here."

Chuckling, ridiculously happy, I stepped out of the shower and began to dry off. "Oh," Tully said, now a foggy, steamed-up glass panel between us. "And I think we need to talk about condoms. Or more to the point, about not using them. Because tonight, when you were . . . not wearing one, I was imagining what that might be like. Well, I think I'd like to try that. Having you come inside me would be so fucking hot—"

I opened the shower screen door. Steam billowed out and he was standing there with his head back, under the water. With a sly smirk, he put his head forward and looked at me. "Like the sound of that?"

"I, uh . . . I don't . . . do you think . . . ?"

"Oh, I think, yes." He put his head back under the water, still smiling. "I think very much. After the cyclone, we can have all the necessary tests. Together, like a couple." He shot his head forward again, a new spark in his eyes. "Like boyfriends, because that's what we are now, remember? I mean, we live together, so technically we're more than that, but officially, if I was to introduce you to someone, I could say, 'Hey, this is my boyfriend, the very smart Doctor Jeremiah well-hung Overton,' and—" He shut the water off. "And you could be all, 'Yes, dear boyfriend, that's completely correct.'"

Oh dear god.

I handed him a towel. "I'm sure they'd appreciate the insight." I hung my towel up and left him to dry off.

"I gotta dry my hair," he called out. "No fallin' asleep without me."

I laughed, and finding my phone, I plugged it in to charge before I slid under the covers. The room was dark, the only light coming from the open bathroom door. Tully singing over the sound of the hairdryer was the only sound.

What a night.

What an admission.

He loved me.

And what he'd just said.

Could I have sex without a condom? Was that something I'd be comfortable doing?

I was in a relationship, I countered with myself. And I trusted Tully implicitly. So maybe it was something we could consider . . .

I certainly wouldn't mind trying. Seeing how it would feel to be inside him bare. To come, to give him my seed, to make him mine in that way . . .

Sweet Jesus.

I needed to *not* think about that. My balls already liked the idea.

I snatched up my phone, needing the distraction,

and of course my home screen had news updates. And there, in a small thumbnail image, was Tully in his work shirt, pointing his finger at a reporter, mid-rant.

He looked incredibly mad.

I'd seen the whole thing unfold on the security cameras along with Doreen, but I hadn't heard what he'd said.

Did I even want to know?

Then I read the subheading.

Storm brewing at the weather station.

Good lord.

Who wrote that drivel?

I clicked on it, expecting to read the article, but the video clip auto-played.

"You wanna be careful," a reporter said.

Tully spun around and pointed his finger at him. He was seething mad, his jaw clenched and that vein down the side of his neck popped out. "And you might wanna watch your *beeeep* mouth."

Oh boy.

He really said that?

"You all come here for what?" he asked. "This office is trying to do a job, obtaining information that will save lives, and you're all here for *beeeeep* what? You wanna broadcast footage of a mother dying in front of her kid, for ratings, then expect him to, what? Come out for an interview?" He pointed his finger at all of them. "Every single one of you can *beep beep beep*. You want news? Go back to your offices and wait for official bulletin releases. Or do what they suggested yesterday and leave Darwin. Do us all a favour and just keep *beeeep* driving."

Oh my god.

He really said *all that*?

He defended me. He defended my work and told them how awful they were for showing that dreadful clip of my mother . . .

And then Doreen entered the screen. She was swinging her bat, her shirt was pixelated—not surprisingly—and almost every word she said was *beeeeeped* out.

Also not surprising.

But they did that for me.

No one had ever defended me before.

The bathroom light switched off and the silver outline of Tully's naked form crossed the room before he climbed into bed. My phone screen illuminated him when he snuggled into my side. "Whatcha watching?" Then he saw the screen. "Oh."

"I hadn't watched it until now."

"Yeah, I'm sorry. I kinda lost my shit. I'm sorry you saw that."

"I'm not." I switched my phone off and slid it onto the bedside table. The room was now completely dark, and I tightened my arm around him. "No one's ever defended me or my work before."

He sighed and manoeuvred his arm under my neck so he could hold me instead. "Get used to it from now on."

I settled in against him, his warmth and strength everything I needed. So much had happened today, it was hard for me to get my head around the gravity of it. From the footage on TV, the phone call with my dad, Tully dropping everything to be with me, his rant at the media, then dinner with his family.

Him telling me he loved me.

Yeah, it'd been a day, that was certain.

And tomorrow was day one. Tropical Cyclone Hazer would begin its descent into Australian waters tomorrow, and we'd begin to see rain, winds, sea swells, and rising waters by tomorrow night.

Then it'd be a full twenty-four hours of hell, probably.

As if his mind had taken him to similar places, Tully tightened his arm around me and kissed the side of my head. "Get some sleep. We're gonna need it."

CHAPTER SEVEN

TULLY

Jeremiah was in the shower early; it wasn't even five. He'd slept fitfully at best, tossing and turning most of the night.

I know this because I did too.

I went downstairs, flipped the light switch and sighed when I saw the view to the ocean was gone, boarded up.

The reason for the lack of sleep . . .

Hazer was coming.

I filled the water tank on the coffee machine and turned it on and set about makin' two coffees. And some eggs on toast. I knew there'd be little chance of Jeremiah eating today, so I had to put some food in his belly.

He came down the stairs just as I was plating it up. "Oh," he said, looking at the spread on the table. "You didn't have to do this."

"I wanted to," I said, putting our plates down. "For my boyfriend, the man I love."

He sputtered and blushed and sat down, speechless apparently.

"I told you I'll tell you all the time," I said, givin' him one of those grins I knew he secretly loved. "Eat up. You've got a big day."

"We all do," he said quietly. "It's not too late to leave, you know."

I ignored that and squirted tomato sauce over my eggs.

The utter silence from across the table made me look up. Jeremiah was gawping at my plate. Horrified.

It made me laugh. "He who has not tried it shall not judge."

"I'm trying very hard not to judge," he said flatly. "Though I'm beginning to question your taste."

"My taste also includes you."

"That's why I'm questioning it."

I laughed. "If I made some fancy tomato relish and gave it a fancy name, you'd think I was posh." I shovelled in a mouthful of eggs and sauce and bit into some toast for good measure, then spoke with my mouth half full. "But I ain't fancy."

He chuckled. "I can see that."

We ate in silence for a bit, then I nodded to the boarded-up view. "I hate not being able to see outside."

"Blue skies this morning until lunchtime," he said. "Top of thirty-five degrees, humidity is currently a moderate sixty percent, but that will climb until breaking point around six o'clock tonight when the storm rolls in."

I stared at him. "Are you a walking weather station?"

He gave a shrug as he sipped his coffee. "It's what I do."

I shovelled in the last of my eggs, stood up, and downed my coffee. I gave his shoulder a squeeze on my way to the sink with my plate. "I'm gonna have a quick shower; then I'll drive you. We'll take one car, and I'll drop you off. I wanna get some cameras set up," I explained. "Can I use your gear for that?"

He shot me a surprised look. "Yes, of course. I forgot about that. I've been so busy and distracted . . . I should have thought about that."

I went over and kissed the top of his head. "You've been a tad busy, so it's understandable. Now, eat up. I won't be long."

I took the stairs two at a time, had the quickest shower ever, and trotted back down. He'd cleared away the table, set the dishwasher going, but was staring blank faced at his laptop screen.

No, not blank.

He was ashen, grim.

"What is it?" I asked, walking over to him. Part of me dreaded asking. "Jeremiah?"

He looked up at me, startled, clearly having not heard me. He shook his head. "Uhh, there's footage." He swallowed. "And photos, starting to come out of the islands. In Indonesia, the Alor Archipelago. And Timor-Leste . . ." He blinked a few times. "Those tiny islands. They're . . . they're just no longer there. Jesus Christ, Tully. Look."

He turned the screen toward me and it was . . . devastation.

The foundations of buildings left exposed, the buildings nowhere in sight. Palm trees and greenery, whole damn islands, looked like a giant lawn mower had decimated everything in its path.

Debris, destruction, flooded streets, vehicles sprinkled about like toys.

"Is there . . . is there a death toll?"

"Not yet, nothing official." He put his hand to his mouth, his fingers trembling. "These poor people."

"Hey," I said, closing his laptop. "You're not responsible for those places."

"No. But I'm responsible for here, for the people here, Tully. And Cyclone Hazer that did that." He pushed his laptop away. "It's coming. Tonight. It starts tonight."

I pulled him to his feet and wrapped him up in a hug as tight as I could. "You're not responsible for the people, Jeremiah. You're responsible for providing information and data, numerical facts, nothing more. What the authorities and emergency services do with that information is out of your hands. You did your part. When they asked you, you told them in no uncertain terms what to expect, and you told them to leave."

"If they could leave," he mumbled. "A lot of people don't have the means. No transport, no money. All those Indigenous communities in remote areas. Their homes aren't built—"

I pulled back and took hold of his face. "Stop. Stop, Jeremiah. Those who were at greatest risk have been evacuated. Those who choose to stay make that choice for themselves."

"Like you. You shouldn't be staying."

I tried not to sigh. "I told you, I'm not leaving you."

He pouted. "Tully."

I squished his cheeks together and kissed his pouty lips. "Stop arguing with me, Doctor, and come and help me pack a bag."

"Pack a bag?" His eyes scanned mine, panicked. "So you *are* leaving?"

As much as he said he wanted me to leave, he absolutely did *not* want me to go.

I rolled my eyes, and with the mother of all sighs, I took his hand and led him upstairs. "No. This is a ready bag. Clothes, towels, first aid, lube. You know, the essentials."

He was quiet as we stuffed a duffel bag full.

"What's wrong?" I asked.

"I should have thought of this." He stopped, put his hand to his forehead, and sighed. "I didn't even think about the cameras, and now this. I'm so unprepared."

I squeezed his arm. "No you're not. Your mind's focused on other things."

"It shouldn't be. It should be focused on exactly this." He stuffed a towel into the bag. "On you. I should have considered what you need and how to make sure you're—"

"Jeremiah," I said, my tone sharp and serious. His gaze shot to mine. "Stop overthinking it. This is your first cyclone."

"Have you been through one before?"

"Well, no. We've had some come close, and most downgrade before they get here. None like this."

"Exactly."

"I've lived in the tropics my whole life. We get crazy shit every wet season. Extremes are the norm here."

"Well, by definition, that makes no sense. If those extremes are normal, then they're no longer extremes but the norm—"

Yeah, okay, he was freaking out.

I took his arm and made him face me. "Stop. We need to pack a bag, then get you to work. You don't wanna be late today. Hazer will be the least of your concerns with a pissed-off Doreen comin' at you." I peered into his eyes. "It's okay to be stressed. It's completely understandable to be concerned right now. Where's that unfazed scientist who walked us into the crocodile infested mangroves?"

"There were no crocodiles when we walked in," he mumbled. Then his eyes met mine. "I didn't have you then. I didn't have these feelings then. I mean, maybe I did, but this is different."

I put my hand to his cheek. "We'll be okay. And you did have me back then. You had me long before then." I gave him a quick kiss, then looked around the room. "Is there anything you want to bring with you? Any personal items you don't want to lose in case my house isn't here tomorrow?"

He blinked a few times, and I could see him grappling with the urge to freak out again, but he managed to fight it. He fisted my shirt. "Just you."

My smile was immediate and the thump of my heart

almost painful against my ribs. "And you think you can't say you love me."

I was expecting him to smile or roll his eyes, but he didn't. His hold on my shirt was now with white knuckles. He tried to talk—perhaps he was trying to tell me he loved me—but in the end just nodded.

I put my forehead to his. "I know," I whispered. "I know."

He swallowed hard and nodded before he let me go, and I ran my hand down his chest and ribs . . . until I felt something that shouldn't have been there. "Are you . . . are you wearing a bra?"

His eyes went wide. "What? No, of course not." He blushed and shook his head. "I'm not wearing a bra."

I pulled up his shirt and he sighed, resigned. There, strapped around his chest was the heart-rate chest strap. I raised an eyebrow and my smile widened. "Clearly you're not as unprepared as you think you are."

He rolled his eyes. "We should get going. Or Doreen will take her bat to me."

"If she does, at least the paramedics will know your ECG stats."

He ignored that, took one last look around my room, at the photos on the wall, and I went to close the door, but Jeremiah stopped me.

"Wait," he said. He went to the photos I'd taken and took one frame off the wall. It was the black and white photo of a younger me at the bunker. He held it to his chest. "Okay, now I'm good."

I pulled the door closed with a smile.

He was quiet on the drive to his work. He was taking in all the boarded-up houses, all the sandbags. It was a comfort to know people were prepared, and I hoped he felt the same. "See? People are ready."

He gave me a tight smile and a nod. "I hope so."

I remembered the pictures of the islands north of us, how decimated they were, and how it was now coming for us. "I hope so too."

We were a little late, getting to the bureau a fraction after six, but Doreen didn't even seem to mind. She was more worried about what the radars showed and updating alerts now that daylight was breaking.

Though she did look at Jeremiah as he put the ready bag down, and how he stuffed the photo frame into the bag. "Clear skies up until around zero nine hundred," she said. "Then we'll start to see this band move in." She pointed to the massive circular cloud mass heading straight toward us.

"Did you see the images out of Timor-Leste?" Jeremiah asked.

She nodded, her expression grim. "Yeah. I saw." Then she whacked him on the arm, almost knocking him over. "Keep your chin up. There's shit to get done today. I'll be back around four. I'm guessin' you'll be keepin' me company tonight."

He nodded.

"Me too," I said. "I'll be here."

"He won't leave," Jeremiah said. "Doreen, if you could perhaps talk some sense into him."

She grinned at me and gave me a shoulder whack to match Jeremiah's. "Good lad."

Jeremiah sighed. "That's the opposite of helpful, thank you."

She collected Bruce, and with a slam of the door, she was gone.

I wasn't about to get into another argument with him. Instead, I looked around at the old gear along the back shelves. "Can I use some of these?"

"You can take whatever you want." He shrugged. "I don't know of how much use any of it will be."

Something on the control panel started to click and he sat himself down and began flipping switches and pressing buttons, which I was sure he'd be doing all day long. Then the phone started ringing, and he was talking to the Oceanic Administration, so I took what gear I needed, planted a kiss on the top of his head, whispered I'd be back soon, and left him to it.

I went back home and collected my storm gear from the garage and some of Jeremiah's and began rigging up a camera housing unit. I screwed it into the wall on my balcony and faced the camera toward the ocean. I set up the old wind sensor and the analogue output barometer from the bureau, hoping they would be able to give us any kinds of readings—if they survived. I hooked it all up, made sure all feeds were recording, and locked up my balcony again.

In the garden that fronted the ocean, I installed the automatic weather station from the bureau. It was circa 1970s, I was sure, probably left behind after Cyclone Tracy. It was nothin' like Jeremiah's, the one that had been damaged at the bunker, but I anchored it the best I could with the pegs and a hammer. I'd already looked into buying him a new one, so if this one didn't survive —and it wasn't likely it would—it wasn't the end of the world.

Jeremiah always had to be cautious with money, and I knew he'd worked hard to budget for all his equipment. But he was with me now, and I'd make damn sure he didn't have to worry about money again. If he needed a new weather station, I'd get him the best that money could buy.

If we made it through this.

No. Don't think like that. Everything's gonna be fine.

Because, damn, the idea of anything happening to Jeremiah made my stomach sour.

I needed to focus.

Setting it all up took longer than I'd hoped, and I didn't really have time to do much else. All my potted plants were inside, everything was as secure as it could be. If the windows exploded in or the roof came off, there was nothing I could do to stop it.

If my house was still standing at the end of this, I'd consider myself very lucky.

But at the end of the day, it wasn't the house that was important.

Next stop was my parents' house. Dad and Ellis were doin' one final check of the docking yard and the offices so they weren't there, but everyone else was. Zoe and her family, Rowan and his, and Mum, of course, was the epitome of grace under fire.

Rowan helped me install the old anemometer from the bureau at Mum and Dad's. It was so old it measured in knots and miles. If it survived, I'd give it to a damn museum. He was clearly worried, and I was sure he appreciated the distraction. He'd never been one to show outward emotion, but he breathed an audible sigh of relief when Dad and Ellis got back.

Then the focus was all about keepin' the kids entertained and getting the elderly neighbours organised, plus their one small dog and a cat in a cage, which was my cue to leave.

"I should get back," I said.

"You sure you won't stay?" Ellis asked me quietly. There was no joking, no name-calling. Just a concerned older brother.

I shook my head. "I can't. Jeremiah can't leave. He needs to man the station, and I need to be wherever he is."

Mum gave me a hug. "We understand."

Ellis nodded. "Yeah, okay. Stay in touch though."

"Yeah, of course. The storm tonight won't be so bad until morning."

Rowan gave a hard nod. "They're saying the mobile phone network will probably go down, so don't panic if you can't reach us."

"I know," I said, trying for more confidence than I felt. "Keep watching the bureau's weather radar and listen to the radio if you can. All emergency alerts will be broadcast." I looked at each of their faces. "Hazer is expected to make landfall tomorrow morning around nine o'clock. You'll all need to be downstairs in the cellar by six. The eye will pass over around midday, and it should last for an hour or two. It doesn't mean it's over. The backend of the cyclone is almost always more powerful, and it'll be blowin' from the opposite direction. Don't go outside. Don't leave the house—"

Dad gave me a hug. "We know. You take care now. Be in touch as soon as you can."

Mum came out with a bag of food in takeout containers. "Take this. You be safe, you hear? And take care of him."

I gave her a long hug. "I will, Mum. Thank you."

She pulled back and gently tapped my face. "Stay in touch. Let us know you're both okay."

I nodded, refusing to let my emotions get the best of me, but the way she included Jeremiah really struck something in me.

"I will, Mum. You all take care of each other."

I waved them off and jumped into the Jeep. It felt strange to be leaving them. Knowin' my entire family would be together without me was a new and abnormal feeling.

But then I thought about Jeremiah and my need to be with him.

And that felt right.

Being with him was where I was supposed to be.

I drove past a servo, which didn't have too much of a waiting line, so I filled the Jeep and the jerry can with fuel, just in case. I grabbed some last-minute snacks and some more price-gouged bottles of water and checked the time before I got back on the road.

It was eight minutes past three.

The sky was dark to the north—far too dark for the afternoon. A wall of cloud was on its way like an ominous blanket about to cover us all.

What kind of havoc it would bring, only time would tell.

The images of those islands stripped bare ran through my mind, and I drove a little faster to get to Jeremiah.

The gate was now chained open, so I drove straight in.

It was crazy how still everything felt. How quiet it all was.

I took the food and water inside. Jeremiah was on the phone, sounding all kinds of official, and he smiled when he saw me.

Knowin' he was busy, I took the jerry can of fuel and filled the generator that was bolted to the back of the building. I was fixing the canopy of the Jeep when Jeremiah came out. "Hey," he said warmly. He looked like he'd had a helluva day already.

I clipped the last side down and shut the door. "Hey, you." I climbed the steps and ran my hand up his arm. "You okay?"

He nodded. "Better now you're here. I was worried."

"Worried that I'd done what you've been trying to get me to do and bail on you?"

He glowered. "No. Worried that you were . . . I don't know. Just worried."

I laughed and threw my arms around him, pushing him back inside. "Mum packed us food. I'm assuming you haven't eaten, because I haven't either. I'm starving. I was also robbed blind at the service station for snacks and water. The prices they charged were outrageous. When this is over, I'm gonna pay those jerks a little visit."

He rolled his eyes. "It's the day before a cyclone. What did you expect?"

Now the control panel was mostly flashing red and yellow lights.

Warning, warning, warning.

Jeez.

"I don't expect to be extorted or racketeered," I said, figurin' the distraction would be good for him. I began taking out the food Mum had packed. "I mean, I can afford it. That's not my issue. What about the people who can't? What about those who can barely afford normal prices and then, in an emergency such as this, they can't get essentials like water? We need to do better. As a society. I probably should have thought about runnin' some kind of food drop to those who are gonna really struggle—"

Jeremiah was smiling at me.

"What?"

He shook his head. "You're a good one."

I sighed. "Well, I threatened physical violence on-camera, remember? So you might wanna hold off the sainthood." I handed him one container with a fork.

"Your mum gave you all this?"

I nodded. "With strict instructions to keep you safe. And fed. But mostly safe."

His smile softened and he looked at the food in his lap. "Tell her I said thank you."

"You can tell her yourself. There were also strict instructions to stay in touch. There'll be phone calls and probably FaceTimes. They're all stuck together in the cyclone cellar, so by tomorrow mornin', if you see Ellis hogtied with duct tape in the background, no, you didn't."

Jeremiah chuckled and ate some lunch. Then he frowned as he chewed. "Do you wish you were with them?"

I knocked my knee against his. "We're not doing that."

"It's a fair question."

"I wish maybe we were both with them. Together. But that can't happen, so no. I wish to be with you." I waved my fork toward the floor. "*I am here* because I wish to be *here*. Maybe you could stop asking me or I might get a complex for real that you actually don't want me around."

He froze, and I'd like to have said that I was joking, but I wasn't.

He shook his head, a little panicked. "I-I'm-I'm glad you're here," he whispered. "I don't mean to sound ungrateful. I really appreciate you choosing to be here with me. I'm sorry if I made it sound otherwise. I just worry . . . I don't want to be the reason that you're separated from them."

I knocked my knee to his again, and this time, I hooked my foot around his as well. "You're not. I'm the reason. Because stupid-me went and fell in love with a guy who has a pretty important job to do."

He went from pouting, to frowning, to smiling, to blushing all in the space of about three seconds. "The food is very good," he said.

I groaned. "I tell you I love you and you say mmm, the food's delicious." I pretended to stab myself in the heart with my fork. "My poor heart."

He made a cute, scowly smiling face at me, then he pretended to stab me with his fork. "You know what I mean. You know I can't talk about this stuff. God." He pouted and handed me back the container of food. "We should keep some. Ration it out."

I took it from him and put the lid back on. I nodded. "Yeah, okay."

"Tully," he murmured. "I'm sorry."

I should have found some comfort in the fact that he was blushing, and he *did* look sorry. "It's fine. Have you been busy today?"

He nodded. "Non-stop. It's been good, in a way. Otherwise I'd have gone mad. I didn't realise the time until I saw you drive in."

"The skies are dark to the north. Hazer's on his way."

Jeremiah nodded, then pointed his chin to the radar by my shoulder. "And he's not slowing down. Gathering speed, if anything."

I sighed. "Joy."

"Yeah, not really."

I tried to brighten the mood. "It'll all be over, mostly, by this time tomorrow."

He nodded. "Just one day."

"It'll almost be as bad as that time you went back to Melbourne and left me for a day. Worst thirty-five hours of my life."

He chuckled. "Almost."

Then we noticed a truck on the security camera. A tow truck, more specifically. And it came into the yard.

What the hell?

"I'll go," I said, putting the food containers down and heading toward the door. I picked up the baseball bat and went out. The driver was a huge man, and I wasn't sure if holdin' the bat was a good or bad decision.

Until Doreen and a smaller woman jumped out of the truck. "Thanks, mate. Be safe," Doreen said with a wave to the tow truck driver.

The woman she was with, who I could see now was holding Bruce, blew the truck driver a kiss. Doreen laughed, slung a bag over her shoulder, and she turned to see me.

Holding her bat.

She grinned. "I knew I liked you, Tully."

I snorted. "Thanks. Something wrong with your bike?"

"Nah. Just thought I'd leave it at home. Safer there."

Yeah, of course. "Good idea."

Doreen threw her thumb toward the now-leaving tow truck. "That's my baby brother." Then she slung her arm around the woman. "And this is my Suri."

Suri was a small woman with long black hair, Indonesian or Malaysian, if I had to guess. She was maybe fifty years old, tucked right into Doreen's side like she was made for it, and had a beautiful smile. "Hello," she said brightly.

"Nice to meet you," I said, holding the door for

them. "I do believe we're in for a spot of weather. Might want to come inside."

Doreen snorted. "Figured we'd get in before the rain started. No point in getting wet," she said, letting Suri walk in first.

I grinned at her and she rolled her eyes as she walked in. "Oyyy," she said, seeing the screens and flashing buttons on the console dash. "Jiminy Crickets, you a bit busy or something?" she said, immediately taking her seat and helping Jeremiah. "Saw the gate was chained open," she said after a few seconds. She glanced back at me and gave a nod. "Smart thinkin'."

I shrugged. "Don't look at me. It was Jeremiah."

Jeremiah stood up and went to the data feed screen, which was now rolling like a poker machine. "I just thought it would be safer, should we need to leave in a hurry, or if debris should be forced against the fence, it could block us in. I didn't think we'd get any unwanted visitors today."

He went back to his seat and only then seemed to notice the other person in the room. "Oh, my goodness, I'm sorry," he said, getting back to his feet.

"Jeremiah," I said. "This is Suri, Doreen's better half."

"*Much* better half," Suri said.

"Hey," Doreen grumbled.

Suri winked, and then she nodded to the screens up the top, showing different views of the storm. "Oh, look. Some screens that work."

Jeremiah held his hand out for Suri to shake. "Nice

to meet you. And Tully replaced those screens. And he fixed the old chair."

Well, the screens hadn't cost much, and I'd paid for them because it was unlikely that Jeremiah would get much funding out of the head office. The chair was a necessity, especially with all the time I'd spent here with him in his first week. It was bad enough that his office was straight out of the time warp, and I wanted him to stay. I tried to make it as comfortable for him as I could.

"Nice," Suri said, looking around. "It's actually a lot cleaner in here now too."

"Heyyyy," Doreen grumbled again.

I chuckled. "Well, I cleared out some of the old gear today. I set up the camera on my balcony. It faces the ocean, so we should get a front view of Hazer comin' straight at us. And that old anemometer that was on the shelf, I set it up at my mum and dad's place. Oh, as well as the camera feed, I have one of those video doorbells. We should take a look."

I grabbed my bag and took out my laptop. It took a little while to get it all up and running, but soon enough we had a video feed from my balcony, lookin' directly out toward the gulf and Timor Sea, and the doorbell's street view from the front of the house.

The view lookin' out to the ocean was dark and foreboding, while the view at the front of the house looked like a beautiful sunny day. It looked like two different locations, worlds apart.

Suri moved a few things in the office, creating a safer place for her and me to sit against the wall and to make objects less of a missile should we lose windows or worse, the roof.

Then she plugged in some power boards and made sure everyone's phones and my laptop were charging. "We don't know how long we could lose power for," she said, pulling out two power banks to charge as well. "Fingers crossed we don't need them."

"You sound like you've been through this before," I said.

She shrugged. "I grew up with monsoons. But I'm from Banda Aceh."

Banda Aceh . . .

Oh my god.

Oh my fucking god.

The entire province in Indonesia had been almost wiped off the planet back in '04. I'd been only a little kid at the time, but people *still* talked about that tsunami. It had killed over 160,000 people in Banda Aceh alone . . .

Jeremiah turned his chair around so he could stare at her, his mouth open.

Yeah, he knew of it too, which wasn't at all surprising given it was one of the most violent weather events of our time.

She smiled when she saw the recognition on our faces. "I moved here after that."

I couldn't even imagine . . .

"Jesus. And now you're facing another natural disaster."

She nodded with a long sigh. "What else can we do, huh? We just have to do our best."

"Have you been through a cyclone before?" I asked.

Suri nodded. "Yes, but smaller. Not as big as this one."

That didn't instil much confidence in me. But the truth was, not many Cat 5s had ever touched down in Australia, and until they'd changed the rating system, there had been *no* bigger cyclones than Hazer.

And Doreen had lived through Cyclone Tracey. Together they had some experience and neither one seemed the type to panic, so maybe Jeremiah and I were in great company.

The video feed looked ominous though.

"Okay, here it comes," I said, turning my laptop around so they could see the screen. "Here's the rain."

And sure enough, like any beast of that size, dark clouds crept slowly toward my balcony. Wind and a wall of rain marched right at us. Widespread and low, the sheer size of the front of it . . .

Jeremiah's eyes met mine, solemn and sorry. "Hazer's here."

I gave Suri's arm a squeeze. "You okay?"

She gave me a grim nod. "It's not so much the rain that falls that scares me," she said. "But the water that rises."

Christ.

I couldn't even imagine.

"Let's take one last look at daylight," Suri said, getting to her feet and pulling Doreen to hers. "Come on, Dori. God knows when we'll see blue sky again."

I stood up and held my hand out to Jeremiah. "Come on. You too." He winced at the dash panel, so I took his arm and pulled him up. "Ten seconds won't hurt."

I dragged him to the front porch where Doreen and Suri already stood. They were looking back out over the carport, to the north. The clouds were almost above us, encroaching on the blue sky like smoke.

We were only a few kilometres from my house, so it wouldn't take long to reach us. But the winds came first. The trees in the street began to jostle, and the world was eerily quiet.

"Can you hear that?" I asked. "No birds. No noise at all, actually."

It was eery and unnatural, and it felt like the whole world was holding its breath.

Doreen put her arm around Suri, as if the silence of the birds was something she'd lived through before, spoken about before.

Before the tsunami.

I put my arm around Jeremiah's waist and rested my chin on his shoulder, and we watched as the first drops of rain began to spatter their way toward us.

Then it began to hammer down.

And the rain just didn't stop.

CHAPTER EIGHT

JEREMIAH

Over the next few hours, Doreen and I issued alert after alert for severe thunderstorms, dangerous hail, heavy falls of rain, rising flood waters, dangerous surf, and sea swells. The list seemed endless.

Right across the top end of the Northern Territory.

I was relieved that Suri was here because she kept Tully company. They set up camp on the floor in the corner, watching the video feeds on his laptop, playing cards, playing with Bruce, telling jokes, and having a great time while the skies turned dark and the storm raged.

By ten o'clock we'd all eaten, and Tully had had a few phone calls with his family, and one FaceTime in which his mother had made a point of asking me, very loudly, if Tully had made sure I'd eaten.

I'd waved awkwardly to her from my seat. "He did, thank you very much for the food."

"Anytime, dear," she'd said.

I'd turned back to face my console. Sure, it was busy,

and every screen and button was flashing, but mostly so she couldn't see me blush.

Having a mum fuss over me was strangely comforting. Or having any parent fuss over me was, if I was being honest. But a mother, in particular . . .

"Isn't he just the cutest?" Tully had asked his entire family watching the screen.

"Oh, Tully, you look after him, he's working so hard," his mum had said. We'd all heard it. Tully had the volume up over the sound of the rain, clearly not needing to hide anything from anyone. Not anyone in his family. Not anyone in this room.

I, on the other hand, was still not used to such outward affection. I ducked my head, and Doreen laughed beside me and shoved my shoulder. "Didn't think you'd be the shy type."

"Leave him alone," Suri chided her.

Tully laughed. "Okay, guys," he said to the screen. "We're gonna log off and try and catch some zeds. You do the same, and we'll talk again in the morning."

"Okay, love. Sleep tight."

It made my chest burn to hear them speak with such affection. A mix of embarrassment and longing.

"Remember, be downstairs early," Tully said.

There were murmurs of goodnights and good lucks, and he ended the video call. The live feeds all showed the same: heavy rainfall, slanted in strong winds that changed direction on a whim. It was gusty, no discernible pattern yet, only mayhem. A mere taste of what was to come.

"Suppose we should take shifts," Doreen said.

I nodded. "Yes, that would be best. Why don't you sleep first," I suggested.

With a nod, Doreen got up and stretched, groaning loudly, her hands almost touching the ceiling. "Okay, Tully, get up," she said brusquely. "You're in my spot."

With a grin, he got up, taking his laptop with him, and gestured to the floor next to Suri. "All yours."

As soon as Doreen was lying down, Bruce jumped on her, and Suri curled under her arm, like it was exactly how the three of them slept every night.

It was kinda sweet.

Tully fell into Doreen's chair and slowly wheeled himself over to me. "You know," he said. "I deliberately didn't pack condoms in our bag, but there is lube."

"Still not asleep down here," Doreen said from the corner.

I gasped. "Oh my god."

Tully laughed, then pretended to whisper, "You know, I deliberately didn't pack condoms in our bag . . ."

Suri laughed and I wanted to die.

I pushed his chair away from mine. "Be quiet, they're trying to sleep."

Tully chuckled and opened his laptop again to check the live video feed. We had satellite radars and some footage cameras but the one he had was perfect. It was looking out to sea, directly into the face of the cyclone.

All we could see right now was squalls of rain for a few feet into the dark, but if it held out until daybreak, the footage would be spectacular.

If it held up. If the camera stayed intact.

If his house was still standing . . .

And through every minute and every hour that ticked by, the rain never stopped, the winds were a yo-yo of blustery to gale force. I sent out alerts for large hail and some lightning activity, more heavy rainfall, and more wind warnings.

Across the top end, all of Darwin, Kakadu, and Arnhem Land.

Tully fell asleep in his chair around one thirty, and I let him sleep. He needed the rest, and if I was being completely honest, I liked watching him sleep.

God, he was so handsome.

He had his arms crossed, his chin on his chest, legs outstretched. His longish hair was pulled back in that cute little sprout ponytail, and the lights on the control panel were painting his profile in orange, green, and flashing red.

But around three o'clock in the morning, a massive crack of thunder shook the building. Tully shot up out of his chair, and Doreen sat bolt upright, Suri still tucked under her arm, still half asleep. Bruce began to bark at the walls.

"Jesus Christ," Doreen said, picking Bruce up. "That was close."

"We've got an electrical storm," I said, stating the obvious. More thunder rumbled and a crack of lightning ripped through the night, right above us.

Tully ducked. "Holy shit. That's too close."

"What time is it?" Doreen asked.

"Zero three hundred."

"Three . . . ? I told you to wake me, boy," she said,

getting up. "Split shift is supposed to be split. You shoulda woken me an hour ago."

"Well, considering you don't even have to technically be here at all, I thought I'd shoulder most of the time."

She sighed and jerked her thumb at me. "Outta the chair." Then she aimed it at Tully. "You too."

He didn't need telling twice, and given she was clearly not a morning person, I didn't either.

"I'll make some coffee," Suri said, disappearing into the small kitchen. The light from the open doorway allowed me to see where I could lie down, and even though I doubted I'd be sleeping at all, I knew resting my body was a good idea.

Tully took a quick look at the laptop, and his illuminated face showed shock and disbelief. He turned the screen around so I could see, and despite it being pitch-black and rain slanting into the balcony, lightning lit up the harbour like a horror strobe light.

It showed how truly big the storm was, how dark the clouds were, how tumultuous the water was already. And the rain on the wind . . . God help us.

He closed the laptop and pushed it over near the wall, then manoeuvred my arm so I was his pillow, and he sighed against me.

Suri turned the light off, though I could smell the coffee she'd made. The sounds of the storm were loud, and the booms of thunder crashed in time with the flashes on the screens above the control panel. There was zero time differential, meaning the storm, the lightning, was directly on us.

The city of Darwin was getting a light show so constant and severe it almost made it look like daylight.

But the weight of Tully on my arm, his body against mine, his warmth, were like a weighted blanket, and the sound of heavy rain, thunder and lightning, were oddly comforting. And, by some miracle, or a testament to how exhausted I was, my eyelids closed.

I could have sworn I only blinked.

But soon Suri was gently shaking my shoulder. "I'm sorry, sweet boys," she said. She glanced back at the control panel, at the radar showing the cyclone had finally crawled the final inch home. "It's game time."

Tully was now facing me, his face buried in my chest, his hair messed up. I think he'd drooled down my armpit.

Ugh.

I unwound my arm from around him and he rolled onto his back with a groan. I sat up and realised what I was hearing . . .

The wind and rain. Howling so constantly it sounded like brown noise.

"Holy shit," I said, almost having to yell. "It's loud."

"Creeps up on ya, don't it?" Doreen said. "Until you get so used to hearin' it you don't even hear it no more."

Suri reappeared with two fresh coffees. I stood up and took one, and she handed the other to Tully, who was still sitting on the floor, trying to come to terms with the world. "'S time?" he asked.

"Six o'clock," Suri answered.

I sat in my seat and took in the dash, the radars, the

data, the warnings, the alerts, the non-stop beeping and flashing lights. How had I managed to sleep at all?

The darkness of our boarded-up office was deceiving because daylight had broken. I looked up at the screens above the panel. One was from the top of the news station building. It was looking pretty wild out there.

Seeing the radars and knowing what those numbers meant was quite different to seeing the live feed.

Palm trees were leaning at angles, fronds strung taut in the wind, small debris and rubbish swept along flooded waterlogged streets. Water from the bay was ebbing onto the road, the shores and sand no longer visible.

The foreshore and CBD were close to going under as the tide came in.

And the cyclone hadn't even started yet.

The low-lying areas to the east, into Kakadu and Arnhem Land, were flooding. Heavy falls continued to batter them.

Tully opened his laptop and went straight to the breakfast news channel. He turned up the volume.

"All eyes in the country are on Darwin this morning as daylight breaks and we can begin to see the size, the monstrosity of what is yet to come as Cyclone Hazer bears down on an already battered city."

There was a news reporter standing out in the street, like an idiot. She looked vaguely familiar as one of the reporters who Tully had told to take a hike. She wore a yellow raincoat, spoke to the camera, having to yell to be heard over the noise. She was being spattered by rain, the view behind her was of the street fronting the foreshore, barely recognisable.

I sighed. "She's an idiot for standing out there."

"They make them do it," Doreen said.

"Well, any producer who makes their reporters stand in harm's way for good ratings should be fired." I shook my head. "The ratings will be awesome when she's speared with flying debris live on morning television. Great family viewing."

Doreen snorted, and Tully sipped his coffee. "I think she's the one I gave an earful to the other day."

"We've had non-stop reports coming in from the weather bureau overnight," the reporter said on the screen. "Now, we know that station has to be controlled manually, so I'd like to give a shout out to the hard-working team that gives us the information to keep us safe."

"Woo-hoo!" Doreen hollered and whacked my shoulder. "She made us out to be heroes."

I rolled my eyes. "I still don't like her, and she's still an idiot for standing out there like that."

Tully shrugged. "Well, at least she's not here, annoying us."

That was true. "Fair point."

"Gonna call my fam," he said, quickly hitting the FaceTime app. In just a few seconds, the screen filled with a bunch of faces. "Hey, guys," he said.

"Morning, Tully," his dad said. Others chorused in as well.

Including Ellis. "Hey, dick bag."

Then Rowan and two women I'd never seen before

—maybe Zoe and Rowan's wife—shoved him out of the screen, admonishing his language in front of the kids.

Tully thought it was funny. "There's duct tape in the drawers. If you hogtie him, you *have* to send me pictures."

His mum sighed. "So how're you holding up?"

He had to kind of yell over the storm. "Yeah, we're fine here, Mum. How about you guys?"

His dad nodded. "We're all fine. It's nice and cosy right now. The noise above us is crazy, but we've got food and water, and everyone's safe."

"Good, good. And yeah, it's loud here too. Probably a good thing we can't see outside, though the video feeds are lookin' pretty wild." Tully's smile faltered for a brief second, and it hurt to know a part of him, even the smallest part, wished he was there with them and that I was the reason he wasn't.

"So," he said. "Things are gonna get rough for the next couple of hours. Jeremiah, what's the status?"

I didn't want to say specifics because I didn't want to sound pessimistic or scare them. I could only nod and repeat what he said. "Yeah. Things are going to get rough for the next couple of hours."

My eyes caught his, and he nodded. Then Tully smiled back at the screen. "Okay. We'll talk again soon, okay?"

They all nodded. "Love you," his dad said, and my heart burned. Hearing their affection and love for one another made my relationship with my own father feel so . . . sad.

I busied myself with the console, reading some

incredible data. Wind speeds I'd never seen before, lows of 980 hPa and rainfall in excess of 200 ml in just a matter of hours. It was all Doreen and I could do to keep the alerts up to date with the data coming in. But my mind kept wandering . . .

Until Doreen's big hand gripped my shoulder. Gentle but firm. "You okay there, doc?"

Startled, I nodded quickly. I hadn't realised I'd zoned out. "Ah, yeah, of course."

Tully came over and parked himself on my lap. "Tully, I can't see—"

He held my phone. "Call your dad."

"I'm kinda busy."

He pressed the phone into my chest in hopes I'd take it. "While we still have mobile phone towers. While you still can."

"Tully—"

He sighed, then held my phone up to my face to unlock the screen. He scrolled for a second, pressed some buttons, then held the phone to my ear. My father's voice was faint. "Hello."

Goddammit.

"Hi, Dad, it's me. You're gonna have to speak up. I can't hear you."

"Jeremiah? Can you hear me now?"

It sounded like he was yelling but I could still barely hear him. "Yeah, now I can. It's pretty loud here."

"I've been watching the news," he said. "Wondered how you were getting on."

"All good at the moment. The frontal wall is just on us now. Things are gonna get busy for a while."

He was quiet for a second. "Right, yes. I suppose they will."

Then I was quiet, because I had no clue what to say. We were never good with talking. "Okay, Dad. I have to go."

Another beat of silence. "Well, thanks for calling. I would have been worried."

Would have?

It sounded like he was already, but maybe not.

"I'll call you when I can. They're saying we might lose the phone towers and power, so don't worry too much if I can't reach you."

"Oh, sure. Okay, I'll let you go."

"Bye, Dad."

"Okay. Be good."

And the line went dead.

Tully took the phone from my ear. He gave the back of my neck a squeeze. "You okay?"

I nodded. "Yes. Thank you." I met his gaze. "Thank you."

He kissed the top of my head. "You're welcome."

"Okay, we've got two hundred and twenty kilometre per hour winds coming," Doreen said.

Christ.

The roar outside was almost deafening as it was. The building shook with the force of the wind, the roof rattled consistently. We could hear the equipment on the roof resisting, the antennas, the ariels, and satellite dishes protesting, the metal all creaking and groaning.

But it felt as if it'd hold.

I was beginning to think this building was another

bunker, second to the one in Kakadu. Built in the days when things were made to last. Granted, the bureau wasn't built on the waterfront where Hazer was hitting first . . .

I glanced up at the screens showing live footage from the newsroom. The screen looked broken, only showing grey staticky images, but no. It was just all we could see. Shuddering views of horizontal rain and glimpses out to the ocean that looked like a void.

It was as incredible as it was frightening.

But the noise. I couldn't believe how loud it was.

I had to wonder how Tully's house was and if it was still standing. It fronted the water and would possibly be a direct hit.

"Tully, how's your camera holding up?" I glanced back to find him and Suri sitting against the wall, close together, his arm around her shoulder. She was clearly scared, visibly shaking, and knowing she'd survived the Banda Aceh disaster, I wasn't surprised.

Me looking back at them caused Doreen to look as well, and she froze. "Suri," she murmured as she stood, just as the sound of metal ripping screeched in the furore above us. One of the dash screens went black.

"We've lost the pressure sensor," I said.

But Doreen didn't care. The console panel was forgotten, the work, the cyclone, everything else forgotten as she quickly sat beside Suri and scooped her up, Bruce included.

"Jeremiah," Tully yelled, ducking his head at the noise. He patted the floor next to him. "Come and sit here."

More torn metal screeched above us, and I looked at the console just in time to see another screen blink out. "The satellite's gone," I said.

Not that they could hear me.

The building was shaking so much now, rattling and groaning. I looked up at the ceiling, expecting it to peel back or rip away at any second . . . yet somehow it held.

Tully's hand on my arm startled me. He pulled me over to the corner with them, his hand in a death grip on mine. And I realised then—a little too late, like I usually did—that it wasn't for my comfort, but his.

He needed me.

So I put my arm around him and held his hands with my other. "It's okay," I yelled so he could hear. "We'll be okay."

I wanted to check his laptop, to see the view from his balcony, but thought better of it.

There was a good chance the camera would be out, and he didn't need to worry about if that meant his house was gone with it.

"I should have taken the job in the Antarctic," I yelled, holding Tully a little tighter. "They don't have cyclones there, and how bad could a snowstorm be?"

He looked up at me, and when he saw that I was joking, he almost smiled. "I'm from the tropics," he yelled back. "We can't move to anywhere it snows."

I laughed and kissed the side of his head, holding him tighter. I love that he included the *we* part to that.

That we'd be a *we* to factor in all our decisions.

Was it probably far too early in our relationship for that kind of thinking?

Maybe.

In the middle of a cyclone in a building that felt as if it was seconds from crumbling around us, did I give one fuck about what anyone else thought?

No.

This man who loved me, who sat huddled in my arms, trembling and shying from every sudden noise, every bang, every creak and groan of bricks and mortar and steel. At the sound of hell being unleashed outside.

In the face of uncertainty, priorities are made clear.

If this was our last day on Earth, I wanted it to be with him. And if it wasn't our last, I wanted many more with him.

So I held him a little tighter, cradled him closer.

I knew, theoretically, what to expect from enduring a cyclone. I'd read data reports and heard accounts of people who had lived through them. I'd seen the footage of the aftermath, and I knew the power of nature it took to amass that kind of destruction.

What I had grossly underestimated was the noise. Or perhaps one had to experience it firsthand to really grasp what the sound of a cyclone was like. It sounded like a plane was landing in the room. Or a train. Or both.

But the strangest thing for me was time.

Time felt wrong.

Every second was a minute, every minute was an hour.

I could see the radar from where I sat. I could see it still moving in real time, but everything else was in slow motion in almost three-hundred-kilometre-an-hour winds.

It made everything feel surreal.

And I realised then that I was having a moment of disassociation. That perhaps this level of fear had made my brain disconnect the emotional reasoning, and I started to assess the storm clinically, methodically. As if it were happening to someone else and I was simply analysing the data.

Winds up to 280 km per hour.

Low down to 925 hectopascals.

Another 100 ml of rain.

And those numbers, those statistics, meant high level destruction. That meant buildings would be gone.

People.

There would be a death toll. A fact those numbers couldn't deny.

And I'd warned people. I'd tried to tell them when that news reporter asked me.

Had they listened?

Tully didn't. His family didn't. Apparently they had a *cyclone-proof cellar*, but the more I looked at those numbers, and given their house was fully exposed, fronting the ocean . . . I had to wonder how *anything* would survive.

Like the islands that had been mowed off the map.

I glanced up at the screens.

The camera on the news building was gone, now just a screen of fuzzy white snow. And then I looked at the security camera out the front of the building we were huddled in . . .

A sheet of something had been swept into the yard. It looked like roofing iron. And there was rubbish and debris stuck in the fence, and something dark on the landing at the steps.

Something . . . an odd shape. A moving odd shape . . .

"What's that?" I said. I tapped Tully's shoulder to get him to loosen his grip so I could get up. I went to the screen to get a better look.

It looked like a . . .

Something alive.

"I'll be right back," I said, doubting they could hear me. I went into the foyer area and grabbed the door. It wouldn't budge at first, as if it were locked or suction-cupped shut, and I had to pull it with all my strength until it budged, and then the wind got it and it flew inward, almost knocking me off my feet.

The wind . . .

My god.

And the rain, and the noise. So much louder than I could have imagined. Something flew through the air past the building. A garden chair? Part of a house?

But there, huddled against the wall and utterly defeated, was a bird. Drenched, and the sorriest thing I'd ever seen. I wasn't even sure it was still alive, but I stepped outside, trying to keep my body mass as low as possible, almost getting blown off the landing. I grabbed the bird as the wind tried to take me, and I almost lost my footing . . . until an arm grabbed me.

Tully, holding the door with one hand, holding me with his other, a wild look of fear and anger on his face.

He pulled me inside, the door slamming shut behind me. I think he'd kicked it.

The whole building shook.

"Are you in-fucking-sane?" he screamed at me.

The pot plant was knocked over, the baseball bat across the other side of the foyer. Tully's face was pale, his eyes wild. "Are you trying to get us all killed? Opening the fucking door could have blown the windows out or the goddamn roof off. What were you thinking?" He tapped the side of his head.

I shook my head, his anger at me was not expected, and my adrenaline was starting to crash. I tried to speak but couldn't find the words, so I held up the bird instead. It was the size of a magpie or pigeon, but it was hard to tell what it was because it was so wet and ruffled. Soaked to its fragile, hollow bones.

It was limp, but it was trembling.

Or maybe that was me.

I was drenched, I realised, dripping water, and I was shaking. I held the bird to my chest and Tully gripped my arm, none too gently, and pulled me back into the control room.

He all but shoved me to the floor where we'd been sitting before. Doreen's glare could have cut glass, as she was still cradling Suri and Bruce. "Not real bright, are ya?"

"S-s-sorry," I said.

Tully was back with a towel and he ran it over my face and through my hair. He was rough and frantic— my god, he was so mad at me—and he patted down my shoulders and arms, but his hands were shaking and his jaw was clenched so tight I wondered if he'd crack his teeth.

Then his eyes met mine and he sagged, falling back on his arse, the towel forgotten. He took a few deep breaths and he shook his head at me. "That was . . . that was not good. Christ, Jeremiah."

Doreen looked as if she wanted to kill me, but the disappointment in Tully's eyes hit me hard. "I'm sorry. I'm sorry," I said. Kept saying, over and over.

I took the towel and wrapped the bird up, tucking its wings in and covering its head to keep it safe. Tully watched me for a bit, though I still couldn't meet his gaze. He slid back over to sit next to me. "I'm still mad at you," he said.

"I'm sorry," I said. "I didn't think."

He looked at me with *no fucking shit* written all over his face. "For a bird. That's probably gonna die of shock anyway."

I held the bundle of towel more protectively. "No he won't."

Tully rolled his eyes, took the bundle of towel, and holding it to his chest, he sidled in under my arm. He held my arm over his shoulder, looking at my watch. It was flashing, though the beeps weren't loud enough to hear over the wind.

He knew what it meant.

My heart rate was high, and he knew then just how scared I was.

His eyes cut to mine and he held my arm tighter. "I'm still mad at you," he said, before snuggling into me and putting his head into the crook of my neck.

And then the lights went out and the dashboard went dark.

Suri let out a cry, and Doreen soothed her. "It's okay, the generator will kick in."

We waited and waited . . .

Nothing.

The generator had either been disconnected, or maybe it was no longer there at all.

I scrambled for my phone and hit the torch button. It lit up the small, dark room enough that Suri breathed a little better.

And we stayed like that for what felt like an age, until time didn't mean anything anymore, until the winds got quieter. I only really noticed because I could hear over the roar of the wind again. I kissed the top of Tully's head and lifted him off me so I could stand up.

I began flipping switches, trying to get anything to work. The only operational screen was the old Doppler radar.

It showed Hazer directly above us, rotating and not slowing down at all.

But within the span of maybe five minutes, the wind outside had stopped altogether. Like someone had switched the cyclone off, yet on the screen it was still very much there.

And that could only mean one thing.

We were in the eye of the cyclone.

CHAPTER NINE
TULLY

JEREMIAH OVERTON WAS A GENIUS. *SUPER* SMART, graduated early, earned his doctorate well before any of his peers. An undeniably incredibly smart man.

He was also really fuckin' stupid.

Stupid for openin' the door.

Stupid for goin' outside.

Stupid, stupid, stupid.

If it had been for a human, I could understand.

But a bird?

An already half-dead bird, at that.

How the building we were in still had a roof, I didn't know.

I didn't want to question it or jinx it.

My heart didn't stop hammering for longer than was probably good for me, and as much as I wanted to wring his neck, I wanted to hug him even more. His watch told me how his heart was pounding too, and despite his outward calm, I knew he was as scared as me. I wanted to hold him and make sure he was okay, make sure he was still in one piece.

I also wanted to pummel the shit out of him for scarin' me like that.

And then the lights went out. He got up and went to the control dash, flipping a few switches and checkin' the data reel. All of the screens were now black bar one, and I could guess the antennas or satellite that had been on the roof were now a few suburbs over.

It had taken me a second to realise the noise was dying down, like I'd stood next to heavy duty machinery or a jet engine, and even though the noise was gone, my ears still rang with the sound of it.

"He's tracking east too fast," Jeremiah said. "Once he touched land, he pinballed east." He glanced back at Doreen like that wasn't good news.

She got up and basically handed Suri over to me.

Poor Suri.

She looked unwell, stressed, and scared.

"You okay?" I asked her.

She nodded quickly. "I wasn't prepared . . . I thought I was . . ."

I rubbed her arm. "You did good."

She cradled Bruce and scrubbed a tear from her cheek.

"This has gotta be the eye, right?" I asked. Jeremiah gave me a nod, and I rubbed Suri's arm again. "We're halfway done. Just another half to go and it'll all be over."

I was still holding the towel with the bird in it— which was probably dead already; I wasn't game to look—so I got up and found a box on the shelf. I tipped the contents out and gently put the towel in it and closed the lid. I put it down by Suri and she nodded.

"I'll go out and see if I can fix the generator. Maybe it got disconnected from the mains," I said.

Jeremiah was checking his phone. "No mobile service. Towers must be down."

Fuck.

No power, no phone service.

"Can you try email?" Doreen asked.

Jeremiah quickly thumbed his phone screen, then looked up. "Cannot be sent."

Jesus.

No internet meant major infrastructural damage.

Because Darwin wasn't already isolated enough, we'd just lost all communication with the outside world.

I went to the door, almost hesitant to open it, but the silence on the other side gave me false hope.

I was expecting the wind to grab the door and I gripped it hard . . . only to find the world outside was calm and quiet. Hell, there was even a peek of blue sky.

"What the fuck," I said.

It didn't seem possible. Like I'd opened the door and walked on to the wrong movie set.

If it weren't for the state of the yard, the water, the mud, the debris, branches, part of someone's roof, I'd think maybe we imagined the whole terrifying thing.

I peered around the balcony, surprised to see the Jeep still there. The canopy was torn and hanging by two clips, there was a branch in it, and it looked like it had been towed out of a swamp, but it was still there.

I went down the steps, past the Jeep, and around to the back of the building. There was more debris at the rear of the yard, more roofing iron, a tarp, the plastic parts to a child's playhouse. The kind Zoe's kids had . . .

And the small concrete slab against the back wall by the ladder was still there, where the generator used to be.

The generator was just gone.

A rusted metal bolt stuck out of the concrete, bent and stripped bare.

Jesus.

I climbed a few rungs of the ladder, which was more rickety than it had been yesterday. I got up high enough to see the roof and didn't need to see anymore. All the ariels and antennas, gone. The satellite was twisted on its side, the bracket that once fastened it, now bent with screws facing up.

But by some miracle, the roofing iron looked secure. Nothing lifted or bent, nothing likely to become a liability once the second half of the storm hit.

I jumped back down, squelching into the mud as I trudged around the other side of the building. All the window boards I'd put up looked to be holding, and as I got to the front of the building, I noticed someone across the street standing out the front of their house. An elderly man, lookin' a little lost.

I walked toward him, talking through the fence. "You okay? How you holdin' up?"

He gave a shaky nod and gestured around. "House's okay, I think. Is it all over?"

"No. This is just the eye. Still got the backend to go yet. You should go back inside."

He grimaced. "Better go check on Jean and Michael," he said, going towards the house next door.

"Don't stay out long," I said, but he didn't say anything, just kept walkin'.

I trudged through the mud, back up the stairs, and inside. Jeremiah's phone torch was the only source of light and it took my eyes a second to adjust. "The generator's gone," I said.

Doreen's eyes flashed in the dark as she stood up straight. "What do you mean gone?"

"I mean no longer there. Just one bent and rusted bolt stickin' up where it used to be."

She grunted. "Fuck."

"And the roof," I said. "Antennas are all out. Satellite's still there, but it's blown over and hanging on by a screw or two."

Both Jeremiah and Doreen turned to the one and only working radar. "This old thing is still working," Jeremiah said. "That means there's one radio tower still operational."

"It bounces off the Coastal Radio Service," Doreen said. "But it's east of here." Jeremiah's gaze cut to hers, like that was bad news, and she gave a nod. "We won't have it for long."

"I'll try and fix the satellite," I offered, going to the shelf where I'd put the drill . . . the drill that needed power.

Fuck.

"Is there a screwdriver anywhere?" I asked.

Doreen dropped her head back with a groan. "It don't matter at this point. It's all over." She gestured to the black screens. "We got nothin' and we can't communicate with no one." She let out a deep, resigned sigh. "This happened after Tracy. We lost all comms. The whole city was cut off."

I wanted to say those were different times, that technology was different . . . but this bureau was so freaking old.

"We need to let people know," Jeremiah said, shaking his head. "It's imperative that people know."

I was almost afraid to ask. "Know what?"

"Hazer. He's tracking due east along the coast, much faster than we anticipated. He's pinballed, and he's not slowing down."

"Okay," I said, not really understanding his urgency. "We knew that was a possibility. Those people along the eastern—"

He put his hand through his hair. "It means the time in the eye is significantly shorter. We estimated a ninety-minute window in the eye, but that's now not going to happen."

"How much time do we have?"

His eyes cut to mine. "Twenty minutes, maybe."

Fuck.

Suri, still sitting on the floor with Bruce, drew her knees up. "Doreen," I said calmly, "why don't you take them outside for fresh air. I'm sure Bruce needs to pee. And the old guy across the street was going next door to check on his neighbours. I told him not to be long, but I don't know if he heard me."

Doreen took the hint and led Suri outside, leaving me with Jeremiah. "I'll have to drive to the police station," he said. "Maybe I can let them know. Oh god, is the Jeep still even here?"

"You're not drivin' into the city," I said. "You said yourself we've got twenty minutes." That wasn't enough time to get there and back, and god only knew what condition the roads would be in, if there were power lines down, or if he could get through at all.

He pulled at his hair and stared at the console. "Think, think, think."

"What about the battery from the Jeep," I suggested. "Could we rig that up to this console somehow?"

He was staring at the one radar that was still working. It stood to fucking reason that the one instrument still working was as old as time itself. Granted, nothing in here was very new. But this radar was *old*.

"Christ. Noah's Ark had newer technology." I sighed. "And people can still see this radar? This one and only image is the only thing communicating out of this office?" I looked closer at it. "I mean, they know it's us because it says Darwin in the corner."

Jeremiah, who was still staring at the screen, began to smile and grabbed my arm. "Tully, you're a genius."

Well, I absolutely wasn't, because I had no clue what he was talkin' about. But he was frantically searchin' for something on the shelves. "Can you shine a light here please," he asked.

"Uh, sure." I held my phone up for him.

He snatched up the user manual that he'd read, tryin' to learn how all the old equipment worked, and he began flippin' through pages. "Here," he said, flattening the booklet. "Light, please."

I shone my light for him and he began reading, draggin' his finger down each page faster than I could keep up. "There's a key," he said. "A master key." He looked back at the door. "Doreen? I need you! There's a master key for this console to change the settings. Where is it?"

She came back in, looking confused. "A key?"

He turned to me. "That old keyboard that was here, please tell me you didn't throw it out."

"No, I packed it up," I mumbled, goin' to the shelf I'd put it on. To be honest, I'd nearly tossed it out—it was prehistoric and obsolete, or so I thought—but for some unknown reason, I hadn't.

After a quick search, I held up the keyboard. It was that beige colour old computers used to be, heavy as a brick, and the keys were huge and clunky. The cord attached had an old phone jack on the end of it, for Christ's sake. "This thing?"

Jeremiah grinned. "Yes."

Doreen was now going through the old lockbox, rifling through old keys and whatnot. She held up a key that didn't look like a key at all. The metal key part was small and circular, but Jeremiah grinned when he saw it.

"Yes, that's it!" He grabbed it and dropped to the floor. "I need a light, please."

I shone the light up under the dash and he shoved

the key in and turned it, then with a strength I didn't know he had, he ripped off the under section of the panel.

"What the hell are you doing?" Doreen asked.

"The only way to change the official site ID text in the top righthand corner of the screen," he said, "is to do it manually with a keyboard. They would have entered in this information when they installed it."

He plugged the keyboard in, getting on his knees to check the radar screen. And lo and behold . . .

A cursor began to blink on the screen.

Doreen gave him a solid shake. "Jeremiah, you smart sonofabitch."

He backspaced through the four lines of authentication information where it stated Darwin Bureau details, and he began to type.

Darwin Bureau no comms.
Hazer tracking sharp east.
Eye less than twenty mins.
Seek shelter now.

And then we stood there, watching and waiting. The only sound in the room was our breathing.

We had no way of knowing if the message was received. No way of knowing if anyone in Darwin had anyway to see the message at all. It wasn't likely, given everything and everyone was so high tech these days, and this was so old.

"How will they know?" I asked.

"Other Bureaus will see this," Jeremiah said. "I think.

And they should realise what we're trying to do. No comms means we can't run alerts; we've lost all signal. The international office will see this for sure. They'll be watching, they'll have guessed by now that we're down. Melbourne too, because Brian will be waiting to see if I fail. They'll issue the emergency warning for us." He swallowed hard and nodded. "I hope."

And we stood there. Waiting. Watching.

Then, after another beat of silence, in the distance, a familiar and very welcome sound.

The cyclone warning siren.

Doreen launched at him, pulling him in for a crushing hug. Jesus, I thought she was gonna break him. "They got it, Doc. You fucking did it!"

When she let him go, he ran his hand through his hair before he braced his hands on his knees to catch his breath. "Oh wow. What a rush."

I ran my hand up his arm, along his shoulder, and gave his neck a squeeze. "You did good," I said. My heart was hammering, adrenaline pumping. Doreen went back out to find Suri, and I pulled Jeremiah in for a hug. "You did real good."

"It was your idea," he mumbled.

"I can assure you, it wasn't." I gave him a quick kiss. "Come on, you could use some air. While we can."

I pulled him out the front doors and he squinted at the sunlight, and when he looked around, I could tell he found the quietness as weird as I did. It was cloudier now, becoming dark again, but not raining, no wind.

No cyclone.

"Did that old guy come back out?" I asked.

Suri shook her head. "I'll go check on him," Doreen said. "It's old Arty. He knows me."

Doreen went down the yard, slip-sliding a bit in the mud, and I gave Suri's arm a rub. She was holding Bruce pretty tight, though he had muddy feet, so I assumed he'd been for a pee at least. "How you feeling, Suri?"

She gave us a weak smile. "Better. I'm sorry I freaked out before."

"No need to apologise," I said. "I freaked out too."

Then I remembered . . .

I turned to Jeremiah. "We need to talk about the bird ordeal. You runnin' out into the *cyclone*," I said, like that word didn't mean a damn thing. "Almost gettin' us all killed. If the wind hadda come through these doors, it could've taken the roof off and killed us all. You do know that, right? And yes, the typing of the message was genius and you get all the gold stars for that, but I'm still pissed about the bird."

He opened his mouth, then shut it again. "I didn't think. I'm sorry."

"You scared the shit outta me."

His eyes searched mine, filled with sincerity. "I'm sorry. I just . . . felt like my brain detached. I can't explain it. Like it wasn't real. I'm sorry."

I grabbed hold of his shirt and pulled him close enough that I could put my forehead on his shoulder. "No more doin' shit that almost kills you, okay? You gotta start thinkin' of me now, you hear?"

Doreen came out of Jean and Michael's house and pointed to Arty's house. "Just gonna grab his cat."

Ah, jeez.

I noticed then, further down the street, two kids were out on the road. They must have been five and three years old. Unfortunately for them, Jeremiah saw them at the same time. "You two," he yelled, pointing at them and walking down to the gate. "Get home. Go home now. Where's your grown-ups? You need to be inside. The big storm's not over."

Did they listen? No. Did they go back inside? No. They ran up toward us. They were all smiles and very excited, so I didn't think anything was immediately wrong.

"Big wind," the younger one said excitedly, putting their arms up. They wore a T-shirt and a nappy, they had bed hair and had clearly had an exciting day. "Big noise. I cover my ears."

They were at the gate now. Jeremiah stood with his hands on his hips. "You must go home. Which is your house?"

Doreen came out of Arty's with a cat carrier. "They live three doors down," she said. "Come on, kids, come with me. You can't be out here. Where's your dad? Is he okay?"

"He was fixing the roof," the older child said. "It was banging."

Ah, dammit.

Jeremiah began walking back toward us. He put his hand to his forehead. "What don't people understand about cyclones? Can they not hear the sirens?"

I sighed. People skills really weren't his strong suit. "Sounds like their dad's just trying to save the roof, to save his house, most likely. Kids will be kids, Jeremiah. They will come out to see people."

Doreen came back across the road, sans cat and kids.

"Are they okay?" I yelled.

"Yeah, yeah." She waved her hand like she did this every day. "He thought it might be better to stick together. Arty's eighty-seven, and Jean and Michael are in their seventies. Arty shouldn'ta been on his own to begin with."

As Doreen was walking up, a white van drove up and pulled into the driveway. Not just any white van.

Channel 4 News.

Jeremiah growled beside me. Actually fucking growled. Before I could ask him to do it again, he set off down the stairs.

Oh no.

"You have to be kidding me. What the hell do you think you're doing?" he yelled at them before the woman could get out of the van. "If you didn't hear the latest update, take a look at the sky." He gestured to the very dark sky coming toward us. "You have ten minutes to be back in whatever hellmouth you crawled out of."

Doreen snorted, and I sighed.

He was going to be on the news again for all the wrong reasons. I went down after him in some futile attempt to calm him.

"You shouldn't be here," I said to the van but taking Jeremiah's arm. "Come on, we have work to do."

The woman saw my attempt at distracting him as her moment to strike. She came out from behind her passenger door. "Doctor Overton, your message on the radar map, can you explain—"

He shot her a filthy glare. "So you know about the warning, yet you are still here? You admit to being fully aware of the risk, you know you had only twenty minutes when you left your newsroom, you can hear the sirens as we speak, and yet you are *still here*." He looked at the sky, at the wind that was now picking up, at the dark clouds coming from the west now. "You no longer have twenty minutes. You don't even have five. You need to leave. Now."

I noticed then Jeremiah licked his lips, doing that tasting thing he did. And he turned to look at me with fear in his eyes.

But then there was the sound of laughter.

Children's laughter.

The two kids were back, near the gate again, but they were stopped, laughing and pointing at each other's hair. It was sticking up, full of static . . .

Oh no.

"Get inside!" Jeremiah yelled, as he took off running straight for the kids.

Doreen flew down the steps and dragged me, the newswoman, and cameraman up the steps and undercover. Suri went inside with Bruce, and I knew I should have gone with her.

But I couldn't leave Jeremiah.

I couldn't take my eyes off him.

He sprinted through the mud and slid to a stop near

the kids. He had to put his hand to the ground to stop himself from falling over. Then, all in the one motion, he scooped them up, one with each arm, and began runnin' back toward us.

I didn't dare breathe.

I couldn't.

He came up the steps to me, the kids were crying, and by god, the fear in Jeremiah's eyes . . . Then, in the next second, the whole sky went white and silent before a boom of thunder cracked so loud it shook us all, and a massive bolt of lightning hit the metal gate.

It was blinding, loud, and far too fuckin' close. The entire metal fence sparked with a loud bang, smoke pluming out in all directions.

Jeremiah was still holding the kids, his back to the fence, sheltering them the best he could. I had Jeremiah's shirt collar in my fist, not even realising I'd grabbed him. I didn't know if I was going to punch him or kiss him. My brain hadn't decided. "Jesus fucking Christ."

The kids were crying, but Jeremiah wasn't letting them go.

I think he was kinda frozen with fear, so I slid my hand up his neck, to his head, feeling for injuries. "Are you okay?"

He blinked back to reality and nodded. "Uh, y-yes. I-I think so."

"Hey," a man yelled out, running up the street. "Girls? Girls?"

Oh great.

He came into the yard, up the steps, barefoot,

muddy, and pale as hell. He snatched his kids from Jeremiah, holding them tight. "I saw. I saw." He nodded, tears now running down his face. They clung to him, their little arms around his neck, and he looked up at Jeremiah. "You saved them."

And then, as if all of this was merely the encore, the wind and rain started for the main show.

There was no easing into it.

It hit us, and it hit us hard.

"Inside," Doreen barked. "Now!"

The dad and two kids, and the news woman and the cameraman, all filed inside. And for one second, in the last remaining moment of daylight, I looked at Jeremiah.

His hands were covered in mud, as were his shoes, and his knee from where he'd slid. He was pale, his stark blue eyes filled with unshed tears. With my hand to his jaw, I pulled him in for a quick, hard kiss to let him know he was okay.

Then we went inside.

THE ROOM WAS SMALL ENOUGH TO BEGIN WITH, SMALLER now when it was filled with so many people. There were two phones on the floor, shining light up in the room. Doreen sat with Suri where they'd sat before. The dad and his two girls sat by them, where we'd sat earlier. The news crew were sitting with their backs to the opposite wall.

No one was speaking.

I pulled Jeremiah down to sit in his chair. "I'll get somethin' to wash your hands," I said, ducking into the bathroom. I wet wads of hand towel and came back out. He pulled his beeping watch off and dropped it to the floor, then he lifted his shirt and ripped off the chest strap—I'd forgotten he was wearing it—and it joined his watch on the floor.

I took his hands and began gently wiping them clean.

He let me do it without complaint, and his hands were trembling, so I knew he was rattled. "You okay?" I murmured. The wind was loud outside, but I knew he heard me.

His eyes met mine, and even in the dark I could see how troubled he was. "I could taste it."

"I know. I saw." I got a bottle of water, twisted the cap off, and gave it to him. "Here, drink some."

He sipped it and I wiped a smear of mud from his temple before dumping all the dirty paper towels into the bin.

Jeremiah looked over to where the dad was still clutching his two girls. They weren't crying now, but they were still clinging to their dad. "I didn't mean to frighten them," Jeremiah said.

The dad was watching us, very obviously seeing me tend to Jeremiah, the soft words and gentle touches. I wasn't sure if he didn't like seeing two men together or if he was just in shock in general. "It's fine," he said. "You saved them. Thank you. I can't thank you enough. Scared yourself too, I bet."

Jeremiah nodded. "You could say that."

I gave his shoulder a squeeze. "He has a habit of running into dangerous situations with little regard for his own safety."

He glanced up at me and I gave him a smile to let him know I wasn't mad. "Saving people's fine, remember?"

That reminded me . . . the bird.

I stepped over Doreen's legs to near where the dad was sitting and picked up the box with the bird in it. But then I also saw the snacks and food I'd brought. I gave the box to Jeremiah, then handed some bottles of water to the dad and a bag of crisps for his kids. "You guys hungry?"

I gave some water to Doreen and Suri, and taking another bottle, I considered *not* giving it to the news pair, but begrudgingly gave one to them. They could damn well share it.

"Thank you," the cameraman said.

"Yes, thank you," the newswoman echoed.

I didn't reply. I just gave them a look of disdain and went back to Jeremiah. He was now sitting on the floor, so I sat down next to him.

"My name's Jeff," the dad volunteered. "And this is Casey and Presley." Both girls were still lying on Jeff, but they were eating some crisps, so they were going to be okay.

"Doreen, and this is Suri," Doreen said. "And our baby, Bruce."

"He rides the motorbike with goggles on," Casey, the eldest girl, said.

"That's right," Doreen said. "He does."

A clap of thunder and an immediate boom of lightning shook the building, and both little girls screamed.

The wind was back to roaring, the rain was hammering with a constant rumble of thunder. Or maybe the whole sky was roaring. I couldn't tell it apart anymore.

"I'm Jeremiah," Jeremiah said. He had to almost yell because of the noise outside.

"Tully," I said, looking at Jeff. I was pretending the news pair weren't even there.

They said their names, Shane and Lindy or Lindsey or whatever the hell her name was. I didn't care. I still didn't acknowledge them.

"You, uh, Jeremiah," Jeff said. "You knew there was lightning."

"Yes," he answered.

"The girls' hair," I added quickly. I wasn't giving loose-lips-Lindsey one more detail of Jeremiah's life for her to make a story out of. "Their hair was sticking up with static. It's indicative of an imminent strike."

Jeff instinctively patted both girls' hair down. "I was trying to fix my roof. Some of the iron had lifted. I told them to stay inside." He shook his head. "It would have got them. It was right where they were standing . . ." His voice got shaky. "Thank you."

Everyone was quiet for a bit as the storm raged. The sound of it, my god. It was deafening. There was no point in talking now.

Jeremiah opened the box and carefully lifted the bundle of towel out. I almost didn't want him to open it. If the bird was dead, letting the young girls see wouldn't be good.

He pulled the towel back and the bird just lay there. Not soaking wet anymore, but it looked lifeless. Jeremiah stroked the feathers down its neck and its beak opened. Dear god, it was still alive.

I smiled at Jeremiah, and he smiled at me before he began gently rubbing the bird over with the towel. But before it got more stressed, he bundled it back up and popped it back in the box.

Then we all sat there in silence, each huddled to our person, as the cyclone battered us. A constant roar, incessant banging, howling, the sounds of metal and steel straining.

I expected the roof to rip off at any second. Or the walls to break apart, or something to slam into us. Every cell in my body was laced in fear, prepared, locked in fight or flight mode; the adrenaline was exhausting.

Jeremiah and I had our arms around each other, holding on tight. The girls were crying, screaming at every loud bang. Doreen cradled Suri's head to her chest, and even Lindsey covered her ears.

Then, after an age, the radar, the last remaining light on the dashboard, blinked off and back on. Our one last hope at communication.

I could feel Jeremiah hold his breath as he waited for the inevitable.

His head went to my shoulder, I rested my head against his, and no one spoke.

Just scared eyes and flinches every time something banged, or thunder clapped, or lightning boomed.

Then the radar blinked again, off and on, then off again, only this time didn't come back on.

"Radio tower's down," Jeremiah said.

Christ.

Time slowed down to a crawl.

Every minute felt hellishly long.

The tail end of the cyclone was so much worse. Jeremiah had said it would be, and he wasn't wrong.

The noise. The roar. The sound of hell unleashed.

For as long as I lived—if I lived through this day—I would never forget how loud it was.

It started to mess with my head. Like I couldn't hear anything else but the deafening roar, and then like I couldn't hear it at all.

Like I'd gotten used to it. Complacent. Like the utter horror outside wasn't happening at all.

Even the girls had stopped crying some time ago and now just stared blankly into the room. I think I preferred them crying.

Suri was sitting up now, still tucked into Doreen's side, still clutching Bruce. With just a hollow look of defeat.

It felt surreal.

Like the worst possible thing to happen wasn't happening at all.

I wondered how my family was.

If they were okay.

Did the cyclone-proof cellar hold?

Were they hurt?

My heart was thumping so hard it was painful.

"You okay?" Jeremiah asked.

I nodded, making myself let go of his shirt. I hadn't realised I was even holding it, but my hands hurt from clenching them. My whole body ached from being so tense.

He took my hands in his and rubbed where my fingernails had bitten into my palm. "They'll be okay," he said, somehow knowing where my mind had gone.

Maybe he was thinking about his dad back in Melbourne.

I nodded again. "I wish I knew for sure."

Then something occurred to me . . .

I looked over at Shane and Lindsey. "You drove here from the newsroom?"

Lindsey still had her hands over her ears, but Shane nodded.

"What was the damage like?"

Shane gave a small shake of his head, as if tellin' me not to ask.

"What was the damage?" I asked again, yelling this time. "The foreshore? The city centre?"

Shane glanced at Doreen and Suri, then at Jeff and his girls, and finally back to me. "Trees down, roofs gone. Flooding. Smashed windows. Some houses were ripped open. Some houses were flattened."

"Where?" I asked.

He took too long to answer.

"Houses gone, where? Which suburbs?"

Jeremiah put his hand up, like he was telling Shane

not to answer. He pulled me back against him and kept his arm around me.

"Everywhere," Shane yelled. "Houses everywhere." He gestured to the air, to the cyclone outside. "And this half is worse than the first."

His words hit me like the storm itself.

I sagged back and Jeremiah's hold on me tightened.

Houses everywhere.

I shouldn't have asked.

Because knowing was worse.

It was so much worse.

And time dragged on slower then. The surreal time warp went on and on.

Until the bangs got fewer and farther in between, the roar was a mere ringin' in my ears, and all that was left was the sound of rain.

"I think it's over," Jeremiah said.

Everyone sat in silence, listening now, instead of tryin' to not hear.

He got to his feet and pulled me up with him.

God, my whole body hurt.

"I think it's over," he said again, going to the door. He put his hand on the handle and paused, looking at me.

The rain got quieter still, so he opened the door and we walked out. Seeing the outside world for the first time in what felt like years. Seeing sunlight trying to break through storm clouds and gentle spatters of rain.

And utter carnage.

CHAPTER TEN
JEREMIAH

IT WAS HARD TO PROCESS WHAT WE WERE SEEING.

The carport at the side of the building now had no roof. The Jeep was a few metres away and now facing toward us. The news van was on its side against the now-broken fence.

Arty's house was missing some roofing iron and it looked like some windows were smashed.

Jean and Michael's house seemed to be okay. Further down, there was a car on its roof out on the street, debris everywhere. Jeff, still holding his two girls, started for his house, made it a few steps, and stopped. It was missing half its roof, and I couldn't see what else.

Doreen went past him and raced across the street toward Jean's house.

My god, I hoped they were all okay . . .

People started walking out onto the street. Someone further down started running for Jeff's house. "Jeff?" they called out.

"Up here," he yelled back. He put Casey down and waved.

They stopped and sagged with relief when they saw him. It was a couple, a man and woman, and they began to walk up. Jeff glanced back at us, nodded, and taking Casey's hand, walked to the end of the yard.

"Oh my god, we were so worried," the woman said. "We saw your roof go. You were up here?"

Jeff was still staring at his house. Or what was left of it. "Ah, yeah," he said. He looked back to us and nodded again. "Yeah . . . the girls . . . Lucky we weren't home by the looks of it."

They walked back toward their house just as Doreen came out. She was helping Arty walk. He was holding the cat carrier, and he looked okay. Suri went to meet them.

Shane and Lindsey were over by their van; he had his hands on his head. They'd be needing a tow truck for sure.

And now the sun was out.

It was hard to get your head around. Like the cyclone hadn't happened.

But we'd made it through.

The office was useless—no power, no antennas, no satellites—but it had held strong and protected us.

I put my hand to Tully's chest. "You okay?"

He nodded woodenly. "Yeah. But I need to go . . . I need to check on my folks, my family."

"Okay," I agreed.

I hoped . . . I just hoped with everything that I was, that they were all okay.

"Let's go," I said. "The Jeep looks okay. You grab your stuff. I'll go tell Doreen."

He tried to swallow. "Okay."

I gave his arm a squeeze before ducking down the steps and slip-sliding across the muddy yard. "Doreen," I called out. She came out onto the veranda. "Is everyone okay?"

Doreen nodded. "He's a bit shaken up. Jean and Michael are okay. Arty's got some water damage to his livin' room, missin' a window or two, but he'll be fine."

"Good, that's good. Tully and I need to leave. He needs to find his family. Jeff and the girls have gone to check his place. It doesn't look too good."

Doreen came over and collected me in a horrifying bear hug. "You did good today." Then she dropped me back to the ground and whacked my shoulder. "I'll lock the office. Clean-up can wait till tomorrow."

I nodded. "Sounds good. First thing."

She glanced back to the Jeep where Tully was throwing his bag in and carrying the box with the bird in it, and gave me a solemn nod. "I'll keep my fingers crossed."

God, same.

I didn't know what else to say. "Hope your house is okay."

I walked back across the street, seeing more people out now, and went into the yard.

Shane met me at the gate. "Are you leaving?"

"Yes."

"Can we get a lift?"

I nodded. "Sure."

Tully wouldn't be happy, but this was not the time for pettiness.

Tully climbed in and turned the key, and sure enough, the trusty old Jeep started. "She hasn't let me down yet," he said, patting the steering wheel.

I opened the passenger door, took the box holding the bird off the front seat, and pulled my seat forward.

Lindsey climbed up and Tully rolled his eyes. I knew he didn't like them, but he wouldn't say no. People needed help, and he was the helping kind. Even if he'd threatened to punch them the day before. Shane climbed in with his camera. I pulled the seat back into place and got in.

The canopy was long gone, the inside of the Jeep was as wet and muddy as the ground, but it was working and that's all that mattered.

We began the slow drive out.

There were trees down on the road, branches everywhere, clumps of hail against fences, debris in all shapes and sizes . . .

Some people were out, assessing the damage, checking on neighbours. Some houses were torn apart, some looked like a construction zone, some were gone altogether.

"Jesus Christ," Tully said.

There were cars on their sides, some had crashed into each other like tenpins. People were standing, looking at the carnage in shock, walking around in a daze. Most of them were crying.

Powerlines were down, no traffic lights were working, water covered most parts of the roads. Businesses and shops were a mess, signs and roofs were torn off or missing completely. The entire city looked like it had been through an industrial washing machine.

I hadn't noticed that Shane was filming as we drove. The Jeep had no roof on it, so he was getting an unimpeded view, and I didn't even mind. This footage should be seen. The level of destruction, the damage.

If he had any way of getting this footage to the outside world, that was.

Speaking of which, I found my phone and tapped the screen. No service. No internet.

That wasn't good.

And neither was Tully's grip on the steering wheel. I reached over and took his arm, pulling it free so I could hold his hand. He gave me a fraught smile, and I knew it wasn't just his family he was worried about.

This was his city.

This was his hometown. His community, his people, his friends.

And I didn't know if he forgot that Shane and Lindsey were in the back seat, because I'd assumed he'd drop them off at the news station, but he turned off before we got into the city centre.

We were going straight to his parents' house by the look of it, through residential streets of huge, brand-new homes strewn with more debris. He had to drive around boards and chairs and roofing iron, tree trunks snapped like matchsticks covering half the road. The once expensive estate now looked like a war zone.

"Holy shit," Tully whispered. "Oh my fucking god."

Up ahead, there were people standing on the road,

shocked and distraught. The adjoining street was some-thing out of a disaster movie.

It was . . . gone.

As if a giant plough had upturned one single stretch of earth.

There wasn't one house left standing. Just piles of debris and construction materials where houses once were.

Tully took his hand back, gripped the steering wheel, and floored it. Driving too fast by the debris, by the dazed people. He swung the Jeep around the corner, took one intersection way too fast, going straight past his street. I only caught a glimpse, but Tully's house looked okay as we sped past—the front was still stand-ing, if that was some indication—though he just kept driving by and up and over the crest.

Shane was now kneeling on the seat, filming behind us, I realised, across the elevated view of Darwin. The entirety of the damage was indescribable.

There just weren't the words.

The huge houses in this street were still standing, unscathed, like the gaps between the giant ploughs had spared it. Tully drove up the gutter and slammed on the brakes.

He was out of the Jeep and running to the front of the house. "Mum! Dad!"

Oh god.

The front door was open and his father stepped outside, and Tully ran into his arms like he hit a wall. Then his mum was hugging him too, right in the front yard. "Oh, thank god," his mum cried.

"Ellis," Tully said frantically. "Where's Ellis? Is he here? Tell me he's here."

Rowan appeared, holding one of his kids, and Ellis came out from behind him.

As soon as Tully saw him, he sucked back a breath and finally exhaled, his hands on his knees, relief almost knocking him over. "Thank fuck," Tully cried, then collected his brother in a fierce hug.

Ellis was as shocked as the rest of them, and Tully pulled back, taking his brother's face in his hands. "Your house. Your whole street, Ellis." He shook his head. "It's gone. I thought you mighta been there. I was so fucking scared." He pushed against his stomach with the heel of his hand, as if the knots that had been there were beginning to unravel. He was still breathing hard.

Ellis shook his head, eyes wide. "What do you mean, gone?"

Tully held him by the shoulders. "I mean it's gone." Then he looked at his parents, at Rowan and then Zoe, who was standing in the door with a small child on her hip. "So much is gone. The damage. From the bureau to here." He shook his head and his voice trembled, teary-eyed. "The damage . . ."

I went to him then and pulled him against me. His hands came up slowly to fist my shirt and he sobbed, the relief that his family was safe, that Ellis was safe, finally bubbled over.

His dad came over and rubbed his back, then his mum went to Ellis. Her sad eyes met mine. "You're both okay, and we're all okay, and that's all that matters."

Then she took Ellis' face in her hands. "Houses can be rebuilt. Things can be replaced. People can't."

He nodded and wiped a tear from his cheek, then he came over and literally peeled Tully away from me to hug him. His mum took my arm. "We were so worried about you both. We came up when the eye passed over, but then the sirens went off so fast, so we all went back down."

Tully cry-laughed, wiping his tears. "Well, I got a story about that," he said. Then his eyes met mine. And if I could read him at all, perhaps his eyes acknowledged that my message on the radar screen had saved his family . . . "But the story can wait." He looked around at everyone. "We're all okay. That's all we can ask for." Then he looked at Ellis. "Come on, let's go take a look at your place before the cops close it off."

I grabbed Tully's arm and nodded to Shane, who was still filming the street, and to Lindsey, who was standing there like she was barely held together. "We should ask them where we can take them."

Tully's mother noticed Lindsey then and went to her, bringing her over. "Are you okay, dear?"

Lindsey scrubbed a tear from her cheek and recomposed herself, though she was far from her newsreader put-together appearance. She nodded. "Oh, we're fine," she said. "Well, I mean, first up Doctor Overton saved us from being struck by lightning, then we sheltered in the bureau office with them and with another family he saved from being struck by lightning, and our van was tipped over, so then they drove us back—" She sucked back a breath and started to cry. "I'm fine."

Yeah. She was not fine.

Tully's mother looked at me. Everyone looked at me. "I didn't save anyone, really," I said. "I just prevented—"

"Yeah, he did," Shane interrupted. "Saved those two little kids, one hundred percent. I got it on tape too."

"Oh good," Tully said, sourly. "Gonna run it before or after the footage of his mother's death this time? Which is worth more ratings?"

Oh boy.

"Tully," his father chided.

"No," he said flatly. He glared at both Shane and Lindsey. "I won't ever be quiet about it. Jeremiah can save your life, the life of those kids, and every person in this whole fuckin' city, like he damn well did today, and you'd still use him for ratings. Remember what I said about eating a whole bag of dicks—"

I pulled his arm, dragged him over to the Jeep, and pushed him so his back was against the door. He opened his mouth, another rant about to pour forth, no doubt, so I shut him up the only way I could think of.

I took his face in my hands and kissed him.

In front of everyone, and they were all watching, but I didn't care.

He grunted in surprise but slowly and surely the tension and the anger left his body. When I was sure he wasn't so mad anymore, I put my forehead to his. "It's been a helluva day, Tully. It's not over yet. Your brother needs you."

Tully's face crumpled a little, more tears fell, and he

nodded, his forehead to my chin. He let out a shaky breath and regrouped. "Okay. Thank you."

"You're welcome."

Tully scrubbed his face, ignored the news crew, then looked over at Ellis. "Come on. I'll drive you."

They were all looking at us. I had just kissed Tully in front of them, so it wasn't surprising. Embarrassing still, nonetheless.

"We'll be there shortly," his mum said.

Ellis opened the passenger door to the Jeep. "Get in the back," Tully said. "That's Jeremiah's seat. Learn your place."

"I gotta open the door to get in." He climbed through and sat down on the very wet seat. "Christ, did you park it in the sea?"

Tully started the engine. "We were in a fucking cyclone, Ellis."

I lifted the box carefully and took my seat in the front. Tully and Ellis were still bickering, and their mother was giving Rowan instructions about using the BBQ to feed people, while their dad was showing Shane and Lindsey to his car.

When he got to the top of the crest, Tully stopped the Jeep so we could see the view over Darwin.

It was hard to put into words. We could see where the cyclone had touched down, its trail of destruction like jagged wounds gouged open.

Ellis' jaw dropped, his eyes wide and teary.

When Tully saw his brother's face in the rear-vision mirror, he began the drive down. Slower this time. We drove past Tully's street, just able to see that his house looked intact. We wouldn't know for sure until we went inside, but there was no debris and it all looked decidedly calm.

Unlike just a few streets over.

There were more people out on the street now, clearly in shock and distraught, and Tully slowed the Jeep to a crawl as he drove into Ellis' street.

These were once huge luxury houses. Like Tully's, like his parents' house.

Now they looked like they'd been through a woodchipper.

Tully pulled up to one particular pile, getting off the street the best he could. The road was a minefield as it was, but the sound of sirens was getting louder and louder, and there was a good chance emergency vehicles would be arriving soon.

We got out, and Tully pulled his seat forward for Ellis.

He was pale and dismayed, and as he stood there looking at where his house once stood, his chin wobbled, and his hand shook as he ran it through his hair.

Tully put his arm around his shoulders, and for a while, no one spoke.

Then Ellis turned around to look at his neighbours' houses. "The Bakshis were in Perth, I think. Mrs Mahoney left to be with her daughter. John and Rayna went south." He pointed to a house down the road. "But the Lims were staying. God, so were the Wards . . ."

He began walking down there. Then he began to run.

"Ellis, wait," Tully said, running after him.

I began to follow too, but as Ellis got to the next house down, an older man came out with his arm around a woman, and Ellis stopped running. "Mr Lim! Winnie, are you okay?"

I stopped as well and let them talk in private.

I was glad they were okay, but my god . . . this whole street . . . I wanted to do something. I wanted to help. But I didn't know where to start. I was so tired and saddened, and I was so sorry that this had happened.

It wasn't my fault, I knew that. But still, there was a shadow of responsibility that hung over me.

There was no way to predict which street exactly would get wiped off the map, but any of these waterfront homes were a risk. Sure, we knew the warmer air over land would affect the trajectory of the cyclone, coming from the cooler air over water. We knew the science behind it.

But Mother Nature was an unpredictable beast.

There were always likelihoods and probables.

Behind Ellis' house was a nature reserve, by the looks of it, that fronted the bay. The cyclone hit land right here. Not a few streets over, not Tully's house. Not a few streets over from that. Not his parents' house where they'd all sheltered.

Thank god.

Having them all seek shelter in one place had been frightening, and in hindsight, probably foolish. If it had been their home that was hit, if they didn't have a cyclone-proof cellar, Tully could have lost his entire family in one fell swoop. Every single one of them.

Does he know how close he came?

How would one salvage the wreckage from that?

How did we salvage anything from this?

Looking at Ellis' house, I wasn't sure what was left to salvage at all.

I walked into the mess of what was left. It was sodden and strewn everywhere. There was half a wall to the right still standing, nothing on the left, and there was no roof at all. Plasterboard was everywhere, half a couch upended, clothes, papers, a broken table. The kitchen island bench was still there, but the fridge was now laying a few metres outside.

I wasn't sure what I could tread on, so I didn't go far. It was unsafe, and the last thing the hospital needed right now was me being injured for being stupid.

"Jeremiah?" Tully called out from where he was standing with Ellis. "What are you doing?"

They were at the front of the house. I gave him a sad smile. "I know. I just . . ." My foot slipped a little, and I looked down to see I was standing on what was a piece of kitchen cabinet or a dresser of some kind. But I spotted something else, half hidden.

It was a clock.

It was silver and art deco, or some other style I wasn't familiar with. It looked old and maybe it meant something to him. I had to lift a piece of plywood off it, but I picked it up, surprised by its weight, and brushed it off. I walked out with it, stepping over everything, and Tully held his hand out to help me over the last part.

I handed the clock to Ellis.

He took it with a teary smile, wiping the crystal face.

"Granddad's desk clock," Tully said.

Ellis nodded and wiped a tear from his cheek. "It was upstairs," he said.

Christ. This house used to be double storey?

Tully pulled his brother in for another hug as their parents arrived, clearly shocked by what they saw.

"Oh, good heavens," his mother whispered, her hand to her mouth.

Their dad put a hand on each son. "Thank god you weren't here, Ellis."

A fire truck turned into the street, lights flashing, and they cut the siren. They stopped at the first house.

"Let's see what we can find," his dad said. "Before they kick us out."

"Dad, stop," Ellis said, grabbing his father's arm. "Don't." He shook his head and sighed. "There are gas lines, and that wall doesn't look stable." He looked at what used to be his house. "All my photos are in the cloud. My hard drive is backed up; all my work files are saved. I'm wearing the watch you guys bought me." He shook his head and shrugged. "What's left is just . . . stuff. It's just replaceable stuff." He held up the clock and gave me a sad smile. "Except this."

Tully put his arm around me. He rested his forehead on my shoulder, exhausted. I knew exactly how he felt.

"I don't know where I'll go," Ellis mumbled.

"You can live with us," Tully replied quickly.

Us?

It took me a moment to realise that Tully included me. Sure, I lived there. But up until now it had felt like I was only *staying* there. As if it were a temporary arrangement.

Tully squeezed my hand. "Is that okay?"

Okay?

"Of course it's okay. It's your house. Why are you asking me?"

"Because you live there too."

"Yeah, but it's not my house."

Tully sighed and, ignoring that comment but still holding my hand, looked at Ellis. "You can stay with us. For as long as you need."

The fire truck came down toward us and one guy got out. "Hey, folks," he said. "Everyone okay here?"

"Uh, yeah," Ellis replied. "This is my house . . . Or was . . . I wasn't here when it struck."

"Do you know if any of your neighbours were home?"

He told them about the Lims and how he'd thought the people across the road were staying, but the Lims had said no, the Wards had left yesterday. The fireman said they'd go check anyway but warned that none of the street was safe and we'd be required to move along.

"Excuse me," I said. "Have you any updates on the power outage? Or the internet?"

He gave me an odd look, so I clarified. "I work at the Bureau of Meteorology and our power was cut. All my systems are down. I lost all comms. I'll need to relay some data to Arnhem Land—"

He stared at me. "You work at the . . . Was it you who did that message?"

Oh.

Tully snorted and clapped my back. "Yes, it was him."

The officer took two giant strides toward me and collected my hand, shaking it somewhat violently. "Well, I'll be damned," he said, grinning. Then he called out toward the truck. "Jimmy, it's the weather station guy!"

Another fireman, who was at the house across the street, came over. He was maybe fifty, fit, and rather good-looking. "What's up?" he said.

"The guy who put the message on the weather radar about the eye of the storm," the first officer said, gesturing to me. "This is him."

Jimmy's chiselled face grinned. "Ah, the blue-eyed weather guy from the news. It was you?"

I heard Tully grumble beside me, but then he inhaled deeply, which I knew meant he had every intent to unload a mouthful. I tugged on his hand to let him know I had this one.

"Yes, my eyes are blue," I said with a sigh, because that was the detail they took away from all of this.

I shouldn't ever dare to not be surprised. Or disappointed.

"In other *more important* news, do you have any updates on the power and internet outage?" I asked flatly. "I'd like to get my system up and running as fast as possible. The building's intact, but I have no satellites or antennas. I'm sure you can understand the urgency.

Flood warnings will remain in place, and I have no access to data or alerts to the east of us, where Hazer is right now."

He straightened up. "The main lines are down. There's optic fibre cable damage on the cable line that comes into Darwin. I believe they're working on it. Could be days for all we know." He glanced back at the truck and his colleague. "We don't even have radio. Even the CB towers are down. They're working on satellite comms but most of the dishes were destroyed, so guessing a timeframe is sketchy at best."

Right. Finally some proper information. Not that it was great news by any stretch, but at least he was taking me seriously. "Thank you." I turned to Tully. "We should go."

"Look," Jimmy said. "Sorry . . . about before. I didn't mean any disrespect. What you did with the message on the radar was real smart, and it saved lives, no doubt about it."

Given he'd said it with sincerity, I met his eyes and gave him a nod. "Do you know if the emergency response office is open?"

Tully pulled on my arm. "Yeah, no. Your work is done today. Let other people do their jobs."

I pulled my arm free, annoyed. "There are still parts of the state—"

Tully held his hand up and raised one finger. "First of all, this is a Territory, not a state. You're new here so I'll let that slide. Second of all, you haven't slept properly in two days. You saved enough people today, and you almost died twice." He held up two fingers. "Twice

I thought you were gonna die today, two separate times, which is more than enough, thanks." He fired a filthy look at Jimmy. "And you still get disrespected. So you know what? You've done all you can do today; let other people do their jobs. What you need right now is food and sleep, and what I need right now is you. And my brother lost his house and everything he owns, and half the city is gone. So . . ." His bottom lip wobbled, and I knew then that Tully was well and truly at his limit.

I slid my hand around the back of his head and pulled him against me. "Okay. Let's go."

His mum came over and put her hand to Tully's hair. "Come back to our place. Rowan's cooking some meat on the BBQ. Get some food in your belly and then you can sleep."

Tully looked about ready to argue, but I nodded. "We'll be there, thank you."

He pouted and went to the passenger seat of the Jeep, which meant I was driving. Ellis went with his parents, and they drove off first. "I just want to go home," he said.

I was about to start the engine, but I didn't. I turned to face him instead. "Spend time with your family." I took his hand. "They need to see you, and you need to spend time with them. Especially Ellis. Especially today. It could have been a very different outcome today. If the cyclone had been just a few streets over, your entire family . . ." I dropped my head. "I know you're tired. But just give them one hour."

He didn't say anything for a moment and I

wondered if I'd overstepped, but when I looked up at him, he was smiling. It was a teary smile, a tired smile, but it was a grateful smile that made my heart knock against my ribs. "Okay," he murmured.

I nodded and kissed his knuckles, then started the Jeep and drove us to his parents' house.

TULLY PLAYED WITH HIS NIECES AND NEPHEWS, HE CHATTED with Zoe and Rowan—siblings he wasn't particularly close to—he had some quiet conversations with Ellis, and his parents hugged all of them a lot.

We checked on the bird in the box and managed to feed it some minced beef and water. Mr Larson said it was a baby magpie, likely unable to fly to escape the storm. I figured if it lived through the night, we could take it to someone to look after.

I sat with his mum while Tully helped his dad take down the boards of plywood from the windows and they tidied up the yard. The old weather station Tully had installed was nowhere to be found, but that wasn't surprising.

"Thank you for making him come back," his mum said quietly. "I know he didn't want to."

"He needed to," I said. "And he'll be glad he did."

She smiled as she watched him lifting off one of the boards. "You have a way with him," she said, still smiling. "You calmed him down so easily today. He listens to you."

"It'd been a stressful two days, that's all," I said,

dismissing her claim. "Though he does have a short fuse."

She chuckled. "He really doesn't. He's normally very placid. Cool-headed and easy going; it's what makes him very good at his job. He'd be the one to break up a fight, never start one. He argues with his brother all the time, but that's all in jest. Mostly. I think I've seen him genuinely bristle only three times in his life: once was when he cussed out the news reporters on live TV, and two times were today."

"Oh. Well, he was tired and hungry today," I said, immediately trying to defend him. Then I realised what point she was making. "Those three times are because of me? Are you implying I'm not good for him?" I started to feel a little unwell . . . I was too tired to be having this conversation right now.

She took my hand and squeezed it. "Heavens no, just the opposite actually."

I was so confused. "I'm not following. Sorry, I—"

"He was defending you, Jeremiah." She smiled at Tully, who was now bickering with his dad about how he was holding the board while his father unscrewed it. "He's so in love with you."

Oh, dear god.

"And it's wonderful to see," she mused happily, still watching him. He was still bickering with his father.

"Are you sure he doesn't have a temper, because . . . ?" I gestured to him. He was now arguing a little louder than before.

"Okay, maybe a little bit," she allowed. She patted my leg. "Take him home."

They finally got the board off and Tully dumped it on the pile with the others. Taking him home sounded like a really good idea. "Tully," I said.

He looked straight over at me and came inside. "Are we going? Please tell me we're going?"

I nodded. "I'm tired."

He put his hand to my belly and slid his arm around my waist. Displays of affection in front of people would definitely take some getting used to. Especially in front of his parents.

Then I remembered that I'd kissed him in front of them, and that made leaving sound even better.

We said goodbye to everyone, and Tully got to Ellis. "You coming?"

"I will. Tomorrow, if that's all right. I might stay here tonight," he said.

It was understandable.

"Plus, I'm pretty sure I don't wanna hear what noises'll be coming outta your room—"

Tully snatched the cordless drill off his father and tried to get around the couch to kill his brother. Rowan and their dad tried to intervene, the kids all joined in, laughing and squealing like it was all the best game they'd ever played.

I sighed and gave a nod to his mum. "Thank you for the food."

"Thank you," she said. "Maybe one day you can tell us about the hero story the news crew talked about and that nice-looking fireman mentioned."

I smirked. "He was nice-looking, wasn't he?"

"Hey, I heard that," Tully said. He was no longer

holding the drill, but he did have one nephew over his shoulder. "He was nice-looking. Until he opened his stupid mouth." He made a face. "Errrr, the blue-eyed weatherman, said the brown-eyed fireman. What a dick."

"Tully," Zoe chided. "Language."

"How come you noticed his eye colour?" I asked.

"Yeah, Tully," Ellis chimed in. "How come you noticed?"

Tully was about to have another go at Ellis, but Ellis was under a pile of nieces and nephews, and he was smiling for the first time since we'd got back. Tully added another kid to the pile, and with a smile aimed at his mum, we took the box with the bird in it and went home.

It was still daylight outside, but his house was completely boarded up and pitch-black inside. He shone his phone torch around, and everything was just as he'd left it.

No broken windows, no damage.

Not that we could see, anyway. There was certainly no missing roof and demolished house like Ellis' and countless other people's.

We were so very lucky.

Tomorrow we would learn more about the widespread damage, and the death toll numbers would start to come in.

But for now, like the boarded-up windows, we could block it out and, for a few hours at least, pretend the outside world didn't exist.

We put the box with the bird in it on the floor.

"Good luck, little guy," Tully said quietly. Then he led me upstairs. "No power also means no air conditioning," he said. "But it also means no hot water. Hell, I don't even know if we have cold water." He led me straight into his bathroom and put his phone torch up on the sink. "Quickest shower ever, then bed. And I can't believe I'm going to say this, but I'm too tired for sex."

I snorted. "Honestly, same."

He pulled his shirt off. "But not too tired for kisses or cuddles." Then he pulled *my* shirt off. "Right?"

"Right."

He stopped, and putting his head on my chest, he fell against me. I was quick to hold him up. Apparently the cuddles were starting early.

"Thank you," he murmured. "For making me go back to Mum and Dad's. You were right."

"I usually am."

He snorted, barely able to keep his eyes open. I rubbed his back and he got heavier in my arms. "Just wanna stay like this."

"You'll appreciate a shower."

"I'll appreciate you washing me."

I kissed the side of his head. "Okay."

I turned the water on, and yes, there was cold water. No hot. But this was Darwin; the cold water was warm anyway. For me at least. I lured Tully under the showerhead and began to soap us both up.

Scrubbing the dirt, the mud, and the awful day away felt so good—kissing him softly, his lips, his nose, his eyelids—felt heavenly. But exhaustion was setting in, and when Tully swayed on his feet, I shut the water off.

I towel-dried us off the best I could, then helped Tully into bed. I climbed in after him and he wrapped himself around me.

"M' hair's still wet."

"I don't care."

"Been a day," he mumbled. "Thankful we're okay."

I kissed his forehead. "Me too."

"Love you."

His words both thrilled me and calmed me, and even after the day we'd had, I was still too scared to say them back.

I wanted to tell him I loved him. I wanted to say the words so much, but my staccato heart stopped me. Could I run out into a lightning storm without hesitating? Sure. Could I put myself in danger without fear? Sure.

Could I say those three little words out loud?

No.

Instead, I tightened my arms around him and tilted his face up so I could kiss his lips.

"Me too."

CHAPTER ELEVEN
TULLY

I slept like a log. After the week we'd had and the stress of it all—after hunkering down and bein' all tensed up for hours—I was so exhausted. Then in my darkened bedroom—without one sliver of light and having a Jeremiah-sized pillow—I don't think I even moved once.

Not until someone bangin' on the front door woke me up. I pulled on some shorts and went downstairs. "Yeah, hold up. I'm coming." Then I remembered the day before and the cyclone, and I wondered if someone was hurt. "I'm coming."

"I bet that's what he said," Ellis called out. "You better not be naked, for the love of god."

I sighed and opened the door to find my parents and Ellis standing there in bright daylight. It hurt my eyes. "Christ. What time is it?"

"It's after eight," Mum said as they walked in.

"Eight o'clock?"

They got as far as the foyer. "God, it's like a cave in

here," Dad said. "No wonder you don't know what time it is."

I scrubbed my hand through my hair and stretched my back before shuffling into the kitchen and flicking the coffee machine on . . .

Goddammit.

"No power means no coffee," I said, putting my head on the kitchen counter. "I hate this already."

"Let's get these boards off the windows," Dad said, getting straight to work.

I sighed. "I'll go wake Jeremiah."

I took the stairs and climbed onto the bed, crawlin' over to his body and kissing his shoulder. "Hey, sleepyhead," I murmured. He mumbled and groaned. "My parents are here, and it's after eight. Doreen'll be wondering where you are."

He shot up. "Eight o'clock?"

I laughed and got off the bed. "I'd offer to make you coffee, but I can't."

He scrambled out of bed. "Doreen's going to kill me." He stopped, confused. "Why is it so dark?" Then his shoulders sagged, as if he just remembered the whole cyclone thing like I had just a few minutes ago. "Oh."

"Dad's here to help me take the boards off."

He pulled on some shorts. I loved that he hated underwear. "I wish I could help," he said, plucking a T-shirt off a hanger and pulling it over his head. "Doreen's going to be so mad."

I laughed. "No she won't."

He dashed into the bathroom to scrub his face and

brush his teeth. "Try not to drink the water," I said. "We'll need to boil it from now on."

He paused with his toothbrush in his hand. "Oh, yes. Of course."

It made me smile that he was so stinkin' smart, so switched on about all the genius stuff, but sometimes the basic stuff was lost on him. It was cute. "I'll see if I can find us something to eat," I said, leaving him to it.

I went back downstairs to some sunlight coming through the back glass door. Dad and Ellis already had one board off the panel. Mum was in the kitchen with some Weet-Bix on the counter. "The milk in your fridge will still be good for now. You may as well use it."

Jeremiah came down the stairs with his boots in his hand. "Morning," he said. "I'm really sorry I can't stay. Doreen's going to murder me."

"Call her Dori," I said with a grin. "Just to see what she does."

Jeremiah stared at me, aghast. "I'll do no such thing. I like my teeth where they are."

I snorted. "You talk like she's gone Lord-of-the-Flies mode and will have your head on a pike at the gate to warn off those less worthy." I turned to my mum. "Doreen is like seventy years old."

He pulled on one boot and stared at me. "Seventy, yes. But she has a shaved head, rides a motorbike and wields a baseball bat, and wears vagina shirts."

I laughed but he went a shade of horrified pale and could barely look at my mother. "I'm so sorry."

Mum shrugged. "I like the sound of her."

I made him some Weet-Bix and pushed the bowl

toward him. "You have time to eat. I promise you, Doreen won't be mad. After yesterday, you could do or say anything and she won't care. She was in awe of you yesterday."

He pouted a little, which was hella cute. But he shook off his embarrassment about the vagina comment, pulled on his other boot, and spotted the box on the floor. "Oh, have we checked on the bird this morning?"

He picked the box up and slid it onto the counter and folded back the lid. "Is it still alive?" I asked.

Jeremiah reached in and picked up a very alive, very alert bird. "He sure is."

It squawked and opened its beak, and Jeremiah cradled it to his chest. "It's okay, little one. Don't be stressed." Then he looked at me. "What do we do with it? Is there someone we can take it to?"

I couldn't help but smile at him. "Maybe we should keep him for another day or two, just to be sure. I've got minced meat and stuff in the fridge that needs to be used."

Jeremiah made an uncertain face. "Are you sure?"

The way he was cradlin' it, being so damn cute. God, it gave me butterflies. "Yeah. I'm sure."

Mum was smiling fondly at me, and I knew what she saw. Me gettin' all bent out of shape over him. I shrugged because there was no point in denying it. I pushed the plate again. "Jeremiah, please eat something," I said.

He handed the bird to me and shovelled in a few mouthfuls of breakfast before putting his plate in the sink.

"I really have to go. I'm sorry I can't help today. Hopefully the roads are clear and they restore some power soon." Then he made a face. "And if the news crew are there again, maybe Doreen will be mad at them instead."

I hadn't thought of that . . .

"If those arseholes are there again, you call me."

He fished his phone out of his pocket and tapped the screen. "I would if I could, but we still have no service."

Goddammit.

"Maybe I should come with you."

He shook his head. "I'll be fine. They'll have enough stories to cover without bothering me. I'm old news. And I'm sure you have enough to do at your work."

Mum waved her hand. "Your father's already been down this morning. There's some minor damage. Mostly water damage, but the loading docks look okay. The engineers will need to assess them, of course."

Shit.

I put my hand to my forehead. I hadn't even thought about my work.

Guilt hit me hard because I *should* have thought about it. I should have considered my parents' lifework. "Mum, I'm sorry. I didn't even think. Are we able to go down today? Is the admin building okay?"

She patted my arm. "It's fine. You've had enough to worry about. We'll go back after we've finished here."

That didn't make me feel any better.

Jeremiah took the keys to the Jeep. "I have to go. I'll come back as fast as I can and help with whatever's needed. I doubt there's much I can do at the office anyway, apart from cleaning up and assessing the damage. But without power or radio signals or internet, there's not much I can do at all. But I told Doreen I'd be back first thing."

"It's okay," I said. "Be careful."

"Always am."

"That's a lie."

He opened his mouth, then shut it again. "Well, I'll try to be."

I smiled at him again. "At least promise me you won't try to die today."

He sighed. "I don't try . . . It's not deliberate. I simply—"

"Jeremiah," I said, walking up to him. Still holding the bird to my chest, I leaned up on my toes and kissed him. "Have a good day. Be careful out there. I love you."

His eyes went wide, and his whole face went red. He glanced over at my mother. "Tully," he hissed.

I laughed. "Tell Doreen I said hello. And I hope Suri's okay today."

He mumbled something as he backed out, and he turned for the door. He looked back and waved, completely flustered, then made a quick exit.

I laughed, and Mum clucked her tongue at me. "Leave the poor boy alone."

I sighed happily—who would've known that being in love was such a fucking rush—and I went out onto the balcony to see if Dad and Ellis needed some help.

"My god, the sea is so calm," I said. Sure, the palm trees were a mess, but the bay was like glass.

Ellis put one piece of plyboard against the wall. "Crazy, huh?"

"How are you this morning?" I asked.

He shrugged. "Yeah, I'm okay. Luckily I took a bag with a change of clothes to Mum and Dad's, and my toothbrush. Everything I own fits in a backpack, but I'm okay."

I clapped his shoulder. "You're good to stay here for however long you need. My wardrobe's yours until we can get you some new stuff."

He gave me a smile and nodded. "Yeah, thanks. I know you and Jeremiah just moved in together, so if you'd rather I stayed at Mum and Dad's, I'd totally get it."

"What?" I looked at him funny. "Dude. Jeremiah and I are fine. Sure, it's kinda new, but don't worry about it. No one expected your house to be demolished, Ellis. It's fine."

He seemed mollified, then nodded to the bird I was still holding. "Still got your bird, I see."

"Mm. He looks kinda bright-eyed this morning. Needs some food though."

"Are you gonna help us do your windows?" Ellis asked.

"But you're doing a stellar job without me," I said. "I need to feed this little guy."

Mum came out and took the bird. "I'll feed him. You do what you're told. And no fighting."

Ellis laughed. "Go and put a shirt on and some

underwear. Jesus, if you freeball it around the house, maybe I will live at Mum and Dad's."

I tried to kick him. "Stop lookin' at my junk."

Dad stood up straight, the drill in his hand. "The battery in this drill has about five minutes left in it, and so help me god, I will use it on the both of you. Now shut up and help me."

We both shut up and helped him.

Ellis made a face from the other end of the plyboard and stuck out his tongue.

I snorted. "You living here is going to be so much fun."

He smiled at me, and we both started to laugh.

I WAS SURPRISED WHEN JEREMIAH TURNED UP AT MY WORK just after three o'clock. We'd been cleaning up at the docks and the admin building for hours, but I thought for sure he'd be gone until dark.

I was on the end of a broom when Rowan had called my name and nodded toward the car park. I looked up to see Jeremiah walking my way, and damn, it made my heart skip a beat.

"Uh, hello, stranger," I said, grinning. "While you *are* incredibly gorgeous, I won't be buying anything you're selling, as I already have a boyfriend."

Jeremiah rolled his eyes, but his cheeks bloomed with colour.

"Please tell me he never used that on you," Rowan said. "God, Tully, that was terrible."

I laughed, still grinning at Jeremiah. Rowan didn't need to know that Jeremiah had used that line on me, and it wasn't terrible because it totally worked. "I didn't think I'd see you till later."

"I went past your place and you weren't there. Ellis' street is all blocked off and your car wasn't at your parents' house." He shrugged. "This is the only other place I know in Darwin."

Aww. I stepped in close. "Well, I'm glad you found me." Then I handed him the broom. "They've been makin' me work all day."

He pushed the broom back to me. "Good."

Rowan laughed and pointed his chin to Jeremiah. "I like him."

I sighed. "Nobody loves me anymore." Clearly, pouting wasn't getting me anywhere. "How did you go today? Was Doreen mad?"

"No. She was happy to see me, actually. It was disconcerting, to be honest. A little frightening."

I snorted.

"Suri was there. She was much better today. Jeff and his girls are going to stay with his sister, I think. And Doreen had to stop old Arty from climbing a ladder onto his roof, because that's what anyone who's almost ninety should be doing." Jeremiah rolled his eyes. "We mostly did clean-up and damage reports. We have no antennas, no satellite, nothing." He frowned and half shrugged. "I don't know what we can do. We have nothing to work with. Nothing even to start from."

He looked out toward the docks and shrugged

again, like he had something to say but couldn't find the words to say it.

"Hey," I whispered, taking his hand. "You'll be fine. You and Doreen are two of the most resourceful people I know. You'll be back up and running in no time."

His eyes cut to mine, and there was sadness in the striking blue. "What if they send me back?"

Back?

"Back where?"

"To Melbourne. Or to somewhere else? To another office somewhere."

A bomb of rage and fear detonated in my chest. Instantaneous, panicky, and seeping hot. The thought of him leaving, even the mere mention of it, had my blood boiling.

"They won't. They better fuckin' not."

"They didn't exactly give me a choice for this post, did they? They couldn't ship me off fast enough—"

"Then you tell them no," I snapped. "You be the Doctor Jeremiah fucking Overton I know, who tells people how shit's gonna go down. If they thought you were difficult before—if they thought *I* was difficult before—they haven't seen nothin' yet." I dropped the broom and poked him in the chest. "You kicked arse yesterday. You were fuckin' brilliant, and you saved lives, and that's why there isn't anyone better for the job here than you."

He put his hand to my neck. "Tully," he murmured.

I shook my head. "You can't leave. You have to be here. I just found you."

He smiled at that. "I don't want to leave. But I'm

almost glad we have no communication with Melbourne or Canberra. That way they can't tell me that I'm needed elsewhere."

"If they do, I will walk to Melbourne, if I have to, just to crack some fucking skulls."

He sighed and dropped his hand from my neck. "I think we need to talk about your violent tendencies when it comes to me. I'm beginning to think I bring out the bad side in you. Your mother mentioned it yesterday."

Rowan coughed out a laugh. I didn't even know he was still there.

"I'm sorry," I said. "Just thinking about someone hurting you makes me see red. I get so fucking mad I want to rip people apart."

"Well, that's nice," Jeremiah said, making a face. "And disturbing, and completely unnecessary. But thanks?"

I took a deep breath in, then exhaled slowly. "Okay, I'll try to stop threatening people. But they need to stop *actually* threatening you or using you. Or whatever. Then I won't actually need to threaten them, so technically it's their fault."

Jeremiah made a pained face. "I'm not sure that's how it works."

I sighed again. "Fine. I promise I won't threaten physical violence. But you have to promise me you won't leave."

His smile was shy and genuine, and he gave Rowan a quick glance before his eyes met mine again. "I promise.

Though I should add the caveat that I promise to do everything within my power and that some things may be out of my control, and that's technically not my fault."

"Fine. And I'll add the caveat that some things may be out of my control too. Like if that news reader comes back and shoves her microphone in your face one more time—"

Jeremiah picked up the broom and shoved the handle against my chest. "Shut up and sweep."

I snatched the broom with a huff, though my petulance was lost on him. He simply turned to Rowan and said, "Tell me what needs doing?"

Rowan grinned. "I really like you, Jeremiah. Come with me."

I stood there with the stupid broom and watched as they walked inside the admin building.

So I swept the damn yard and picked up debris and sweated my arse off in the brutal humidity until I was done sulking.

It took a while.

Eventually, I ditched the broom and went inside. I found them moving filing cabinets off wet carpet, and yes, I liked very much that Jeremiah slotted right into my family—he was working alongside Rowan and my father, after all—but I'd had enough for today.

I needed some alone time with him.

If I was being honest with myself, what I needed from him was a long hug and some reassurance. But I didn't want to have to admit that. I just wanted to crawl onto the couch and cuddle for hours.

Had falling in love suddenly turned me into a giant insecure baby?

Apparently, yes.

Jeremiah and Dad shuffled the last filing cabinet into the corner when Jeremiah noticed me. He stopped and came straight over. "What's wrong?"

"Nothing," I mumbled. "I just wanna go home."

He frowned and went to put his hand to my face but stopped himself.

I didn't want him to stop himself.

But with my dad and brother in the room, I shouldn't have been surprised. I tried to not let it bother me, but it did.

"Okay, we'll go," he said. "You sure you're okay?"

I didn't answer. I turned to Dad. "We have to go. See yas tomorrow when we're back to do it all over again."

Dad stretched his back. "Yeah, we're all done for today too. Pretty sure I have some beers in the fridge that need drinking before they get hot."

I pulled on Jeremiah's shirt, tugging him toward the door. "Another time, Dad, but thanks. I'll see yas all again bright and early tomorrow."

If they noticed my mood—and I'm sure they did—they never said anything. I wouldn't have known what to tell them anyway. I just needed to leave.

"I'll follow you," Jeremiah said, going straight to the Jeep.

I tried to get myself together on the short drive home, but this feeling, this uneasy, frustrated feeling wasn't going away.

I pulled into my garage and went inside, seeing the

storm clouds rolling in again across the horizon. It was almost five o'clock, and I was ready for this whole day to be over. The box squawked, so I opened it up and took out the bird. He squawked some more and I fed him the small balls of minced meat my mother had made.

At least he made me smile.

Jeremiah came in, put his keys and stuff on the kitchen bench, and gave the bird a gentle stroke. "He's a little fighter."

"We'll need to get him a proper cage," I said quietly.

Jeremiah looked at the top of my head and straightened out an errant strand of hair. He smiled as he thumbed my jaw. "Want to tell me what's wrong?"

I frowned. "I don't know what's wrong. I just feel . . ." I shrugged my shoulders and tried to shake off the funk I was in. "I don't know how I feel. Like I need you to hug me. And it's weird, because I've never needed that before. I feel . . . deconstructed. I dunno. And then you mentioned that you might be leaving. Why did you say that? Jesus, Jeremiah, I just found you!"

He took the bird and put it back in the box, then pulled me against him. He wrapped his arms around me, pushed me against the cabinet, and held me so damn tight.

God, he felt so good it made me want to cry.

"I don't know what's wrong with me," I mumbled.

"Nothing's wrong with you," he whispered. "Nothing at all."

I fisted his shirt at the back, and with my face in his

neck, I breathed him in, like I could somehow absorb his strength that way. God, this was ridiculous.

"Wanna lie down on the couch?"

I nodded. "Yes."

I felt like a child. God, I was acting like one.

But then he pulled me onto the couch with him and I lay there, half on top of him, with his arms around me and my head tucked under his chin. He rubbed my back and kissed the top of my head every so often.

"Feel better?"

I nodded again. "I just . . . I just needed this. Exactly this. With you. I need to know you're okay, that we're okay. That everything will be okay."

He lifted my face and brought me in for a kiss. "Everything will be okay. You and me, we'll be okay."

"You're not leaving?"

He smiled and shook his head, his eyes soft. "They'll have to drag me out."

I chuckled and he kissed my cheek, my nose, my forehead, and tucked me back in under his chin.

Then we heard keys in the front door. I'd forgotten about Ellis. "You better not be naked," he called out.

"Eat a bag of dicks," I replied.

Jeremiah tried to sit up, but I held him right where he was. "Mm-mm. Don't move."

Ellis came in and all but fell into the single seater next to us. He looked exhausted, and he didn't give one fuck that Jeremiah and I were tangled on the couch together. "What is it with the 'eat a bag of dicks' line as an insult?" Ellis said with a frown. "I mean, sure, tell me to eat a bag of dicks and I'd be like, 'yeah, no thanks, not my style.' But if I told you to eat a bag of dicks, you'd be like, 'hell yes, go turkey-mode, and gobble-gobble.'"

I threw a cushion at his fucking head.

He caught it and laughed. Then before I could say anything, or get up and beat the shit outta him, the TV power button came on, the fridge kicked in, and a few other electrical appliances beeped.

I sat up. "Holy shit. We have power!"

Ellis threw his hands up, victory style, then looked at the TV and quickly deflated. "Oh . . . my PS5." He sighed. "Christ, Tully, why don't you have a gaming console?"

"Because I'd never use it," I said, helping Jeremiah sit up, now that I'd peeled myself off him. I got up to get us all a bottle of water.

Ellis rolled his eyes. "Because you spend all your money and time on storm-chasing shit."

Jeremiah smiled. "Same."

Ellis groaned. "I'm living with the storm boys."

I came back with two bottles of water and a baby bird. I gave one bottle to Ellis and kept the other for me and Jeremiah to share. I handed the bird to Jeremiah and reached for the air-con remote.

Jeremiah stroked the bird's neck, and it squawked a bit. It was young and it couldn't fly yet, but like Jeremiah had said, he was a fighter. "We should name him," I said. "Given he made it through the worst of it, I think he deserves a name."

Jeremiah's eyes met mine. "Really? I've never had to name something before."

"Never?"

He shook his head. "I've never had a pet before."

Jeez.

I leaned against his arm and gave the bird a gentle pat. "Even if we find him a home in a day or so, we can still name him. I'd reckon all the vets and wildlife carers would be pretty busy right now, so a few days won't hurt. He likes that minced meat. Which is gross, but he likes it. Lucky Mum and Dad knew what to feed him, because my entire education relies on Google, and without power and the internet, I had no clue." I checked my phone. "Still no service. It's funny how long the battery lasts when you can't use your phone."

"Oh," Ellis said, grabbing the remote for the TV. "Maybe there are updates on the news or something."

Some channels weren't working at all, but we found the local one. Channel 4, because of course that would be the only channel still working.

Footage of Darwin filled the screen, from the street and from the air. There was just so much devastation. So much loss. They showed people crying, people being rescued, people carrying kids and pets through water. They showed collapsed buildings, and they showed Ellis' street.

Christ, it was hard for me to watch. I couldn't imagine what it was like for him.

Then my favouritest news reporter in the whole country appeared on screen.

Lindsey.

I grumbled under my breath.

And then I realised where she was. She was standing out the front of Jeremiah's work.

"I'm here with Doctor Jeremiah Overton," she said.

And there he was. The love of my life, the man sitting on the couch next to me right that very second, wearing the same clothes on TV as he was wearing right freaking next to me.

"You never told me she hassled you today!" I said. I might have yelled. "I said if those leeches harassed you one more time—"

"She didn't harass me. I asked her to come over."

I stared at him.

Stared.

Until my eyeballs dried out.

"When you lost all communications yesterday," Lindsey said on the TV, "you used some thirty-year-old radar that still used old radio frequency, and you typed in the warning about the shortened duration of the eye, is that correct?"

The screen showed the typed message in the top of the radar screen.

"Yes, that's correct."

"And if that didn't already make you a hero, we have footage of you saving two small children from a lightning strike yesterday," she said. "And not just them; you saved myself and my cameraman."

The footage cut to a shaky view from Shane running up the steps, then panning back in time to see Jeremiah skid in the mud, collect the two kids, and race back before the lightning lit up and blew out the fence.

Ellis pointed at the TV. "Holy shit, dude, was that you?"

"Yes, that was him." I went back to staring at Jeremiah. "You asked her to come speak to you? I'm sorry. But why?"

He shrugged. "Because I had something to say."

I looked back at the TV, to the Jeremiah on screen. Lindsey was smiling at him in a way that made me want to poke her in the eye.

"This footage has gone viral," she said. "What do you have to say to the people who are calling you a hero?"

On-screen Jeremiah looked right at the camera. "Nothing. I'm not a hero. I just had no other way to let my dad know I was okay. He's in Melbourne. Dad, if you're watching this, I'm fine and I'll call you when the phone towers are back up."

Then on-screen Jeremiah smiled at Lindsey and simply turned and walked back up to the office. Lindsey stood there with her microphone, not knowing what else to say.

I snorted out a laugh because that was funny as hell, but then I looked at Jeremiah next to me, and with a heavy sigh, I dropped my forehead to his shoulder. "God, I'm so sorry. I'm sorry I didn't even think. Your dad must have been worried, and you . . . You must have been so . . . ." I looked up at him. "And I didn't even stop to think. I'm a terrible boyfriend. I'm so sorry."

Jeremiah took my hand. "My father would have been mildly concerned at best. I just thought he might like to know, and when someone from Channel 4 came to collect the van, I told them to pass on a message to come interview me. They used me, so I used them. I think she was hoping for some exclusive scoop or whatever. But anyway, it doesn't matter. Hopefully my father sees that."

I still felt bad.

"I'm sure he was more than mildly concerned," I offered. "But still, I'm sorry. We got home last night and crashed, then we were up and gone this morning. I barely had time to speak to you, and then I spent all afternoon sulking like a fucking child. I should have been more considerate."

"You were," he said.

"What? Considerate? Or sulking like a child?" I asked, then regretted it because I didn't want to know. I already knew. "You don't need to answer. I'm sorry."

Jeremiah laughed and he nudged his knee to mine. When I met his gaze, his eyes were happy and soft. He was still holding the bird, which we still hadn't named.

God.

"We should call him Hazer," I suggested.

Jeremiah screwed his nose up, clearly not liking that suggestion.

"I can't believe you skidded across that mud and collected those two kids like they do in the movies," Ellis said, disbelief still clear on his face. "You wanna watch out. The Buffaloes will be looking to sign you up."

Jeremiah squinted at him. "The buffaloes?"

"Football," I offered.

"Oh." He grimaced. "No thanks."

I snorted. "What if we call him First," I suggested as a bird name. "As in he was the *first* time you almost died yesterday."

He rolled his eyes, then looked at the little bird. "Naming something is a lot of responsibility."

Ellis groaned. "For the love of god, you two. Mr Percival is right there." He waved his hand at us. "I already called you the storm boys, so really, what other name *could* you call it?"

My initial reaction was to tell him to sod off. And I wanted to hate the name suggestion, but I couldn't. I looked at Jeremiah and he smiled.

"Mr Percival is kind of nice," he said. "Well, it's appropriate. Though he's not a pelican."

"I don't think that matters," I said. I gave the bird a gentle stroke, though he was very content to be secure in Jeremiah's arms. "Mr Percival."

"You're welcome." Ellis stood up. "I'm gonna cook some pasta for dinner. Sound good? The power will likely cut in and out for a week while they fix shit, so we should make use of it."

"Sounds perfect. I can help," I said.

"Nah, I got it. It'll just be veggies and shit."

"Hold the shit in mine," Jeremiah said. "I'm not a fan."

My god, he'd made a joke to my brother.

I grinned at Ellis. "Yeah, me either. Feel free to make yours extra shitty though."

Ellis gave me the finger. He walked to the glass door. "There's an electrical storm on the horizon. Oh, and now we've got power, did you wanna check the camera you had on the balcony? See what kinda front-row footage you got of the cyclone."

I snuggled into Jeremiah a little and he leaned into me, sliding one arm around me, and we both smiled at Mr Percival. "Nah," I said, feeling very content where I was. "It can wait till tomorrow. This is about all I wanna do tonight. Stay right here."

Jeremiah kissed my temple and, over the top of my head, watched the lightning over the ocean. "Yeah. This is all I want to do tonight too."

I sidled in a bit closer, nudging my nose to his throat. "Well, I hope it's *not all* you wanna do tonight."

He gave me a squeeze and chuckled, then whispered in my ear, "Not *all*."

"Oh," I said, like that struck a memory. "Did you check the app on your phone for the heart-rate strap?"

"No. I forgot all about it."

"Hmm," I hummed, kissing his Adam's apple. "We should see what it says. Though we'll need to establish some control groups, purely for scientific purposes. If you know what I mean."

He gave me a squeeze. "I believe I do know what you mean, yes."

I whispered in his ear. "Resting heart rate, heart rate when you fuck me. Heart rate when I fuck you."

He swallowed hard. "Hm. Yes, those control groups would suffice, I do concur."

God, he made me laugh.

Then we sat there for a little bit longer. Jeremiah chewed his bottom lip, and when he started to tap his foot, it got the better of me. "Maybe we could check the app, just real quick, and see what records we need to beat."

"I'm certain each reading isn't a personal best to beat every time. That's not why I bought it."

"Hm, personal bests. I like the sound of that."

He smirked. "Well, I think the sprint across the yard to collect those two girls, sprinting back, and almost getting hit by lightning will be hard to beat. My heart was beating out of my chest."

I met his gaze. "Is that a challenge, Doctor? Because I do like a challenge."

He glanced back toward the kitchen to see if Ellis was listening. He wasn't, so Jeremiah looked back to me. "Well, a little competition could be fun."

"I'm going to make a chart," I proclaimed loudly. I didn't care if Ellis heard. "With gold stars and everything."

Jeremiah's eyes went wide. "Oh god, please don't."

"Yeah," Ellis chimed in as he stirred a pan. "Please don't. I don't know what you're talking about, but it involves a chart and gold star stickers and he's trying to whisper, so I can only assume he's getting his freak on. Believe me when I say I don't wanna fucking know."

I burst out laughing. "Jeremiah, quick, get your phone. We need to check the app so I know how much stamina I'll need tonight."

"Oh my god," Jeremiah hissed. "Tully, stop it."

Ellis let his head drop with a loud groan. "Staying here was such a bad idea." He turned the stove off. "Pasta's cooked. Come up and get your own, nut sac."

Then he rolled his eyes. "Not you, Jeremiah, obviously. I was talking to the six-foot talking haemorrhoid sitting next to you."

I burst out laughing and even Jeremiah tried not to smile as he put Mr Percival back in his box. We dished up our own pasta, and sitting on the couch eating Ellis' terrible cooking just made me so freakin' happy.

Having Jeremiah in my life and having my shithead brother live with us made me so unbelievably happy.

Granted, these weren't ideal circumstances, with the cyclone and all. But even after everything Hazer threw at us, with all the devastation and the loss, to still be able to sit around and joke and laugh with each other, we were pretty damn lucky too.

"Cheers," I said, tapping my bottle of water to Ellis'. "To surviving cyclones." Then I tapped Jeremiah's. "And to more storms in the future."

Ellis shoved a forkful of pasta in his mouth, then spoke with his mouth full. "You're both crazy."

I laughed. "Maybe. But he's my kind of crazy."

Ellis ignored my sappiness and shook his head at Jeremiah. "I still can't believe you saved those kids from that lightning strike."

"I'm not surprised one bit," I said. "We have footage of him running a hundred metres in the rain and sliding under the wall at the bunker like an action-movie hero."

Jeremiah's cheeks were now a vivid pink.

Such a contrast, from the hero to the shy guy . . .

"About the footage," Jeremiah said.

"The footage from the bunker?"

"No, the footage from your balcony, looking at the

cyclone." He shrugged. "Maybe we could take a little look."

I grinned at him. *Hell yes, we could.* "We could hook it up to the TV and watch it on the big screen!" I ditched my pasta and stood up. "I'll go get it."

Ellis groaned. "Oh my god, I'm living with storm nerds."

"Shut up, nut sac," I yelled out.

"Grab me a beer on your way back," he replied.

I grabbed three bottles, and a few minutes later, the three of us settled on the couch with our beers, my head on Jeremiah's shoulder. "Are we ready?" I asked, pointing the remote control at the TV.

Jeremiah kissed the top of my head. "Always."

THE END

THE STORM BOYS SERIES

Want to read more of Tully and Jeremiah's story?

Outrun the Rain

Into the Tempest

Touch the Lightning

Or where it all began with Paul and Derek

Second Chance at First Love

THE STORM BOYS SERIES

ABOUT THE AUTHOR

N.R. Walker is an Australian author, who loves her genre of gay romance. She loves writing and spends far too much time doing it, but wouldn't have it any other way.

She is many things: a mother, a wife, a sister, a writer. She has pretty, pretty boys who live in her head, who don't let her sleep at night unless she gives them life with words.

She likes it when they do dirty, dirty things… but likes it even more when they fall in love.

She used to think having people in her head talking to her was weird, until one day she happened across other writers who told her it was normal.

She's been writing ever since…

ALSO BY N.R. WALKER

Blind Faith

Through These Eyes (Blind Faith #2)

Blindside: Mark's Story (Blind Faith #3)

Ten in the Bin

Gay Sex Club Stories 1

Gay Sex Club Stories 2

Point of No Return – Turning Point #1

Breaking Point – Turning Point #2

Starting Point – Turning Point #3

Element of Retrofit – Thomas Elkin Series #1

Clarity of Lines – Thomas Elkin Series #2

Sense of Place – Thomas Elkin Series #3

Taxes and TARDIS

Three's Company

Red Dirt Heart

Red Dirt Heart 2

Red Dirt Heart 3

Red Dirt Heart 4

Red Dirt Christmas

Cronin's Key

Cronin's Key II

Sir

Tallowwood

Reindeer Games

The Dichotomy of Angels

Throwing Hearts

Pieces of You - Missing Pieces #1

Pieces of Me - Missing Pieces #2

Pieces of Us - Missing Pieces #3

Lacuna

Tic-Tac-Mistletoe

Bossy

Code Red

Dearest Milton James

Dearest Malachi Keogh

Christmas Wish List

Code Blue

Davo

The Kite

Learning Curve

Merry Christmas Cupid

To the Moon and Back

Second Chance at First Love

Outrun the Rain

Blindside

Finders Keepers

Galaxies and Oceans

Nova Praetorian

Upside Down

Sir

Tallowwood

Imago

Throwing Hearts

Sixty Five Hours

Taxes and TARDIS

The Dichotomy of Angels

The Hate You Drink

Pieces of You

Pieces of Me

Pieces of Us

Tic-Tac-Mistletoe

Lacuna

Bossy

Code Red

Learning to Feel

Dearest Milton James

Dearest Malachi Keogh

Three's Company

Christmas Wish List

Code Blue

Davo

The Kite

Learning Curve

Merry Christmas Cupid

To the Moon and Back

Second Chance at First Love

SERIES COLLECTIONS:

Red Dirt Heart Series

Turning Point Series

Thomas Elkin Series

Spencer Cohen Series

Imago Series

Blind Faith Series

FREE READS:

Sixty Five Hours

Learning to Feel

His Grandfather's Watch (And The Story of Billy and Hale)

The Twelfth of Never (Blind Faith 3.5)

Twelve Days of Christmas (Sixty Five Hours Christmas)

Best of Both Worlds

TRANSLATED TITLES:

ITALIAN

Fiducia Cieca (Blind Faith)

Attraverso Questi Occhi (Through These Eyes)

Preso alla Sprovvista (Blindside)

Il giorno del Mai (Blind Faith 3.5)

Cuore di Terra Rossa Serie (Red Dirt Heart Series)

Natale di terra rossa (Red dirt Christmas)

Intervento di Retrofit (Elements of Retrofit)

A Chiare Linee (Clarity of Lines)

Senso D'appartenenza (Sense of Place)

Spencer Cohen Serie (including Yanni's Story)

Punto di non Ritorno (Point of No Return)

Punto di Rottura (Breaking Point)

Punto di Partenza (Starting Point)

Imago (Imago)

Imagines

Il desiderio di un soldato (A Soldier's Wish)

Scambiato (Switched)

Tallowwood

The Hate You Drink

Ho trovato te (Finders Keepers)

Cuori d'argilla (Throwing Hearts)

Galassie e Oceani (Galaxies and Oceans)

Il peso di tut (The Weight of it All)

FRENCH

Confiance Aveugle (Blind Faith)

A travers ces yeux: Confiance Aveugle 2 (Through These Eyes)

Aveugle: Confiance Aveugle 3 (Blindside)

À Jamais (Blind Faith 3.5)

Cronin's Key Series

Au Coeur de Sutton Station (Red Dirt Heart)

Partir ou rester (Red Dirt Heart 2)

Faire Face (Red Dirt Heart 3)

Trouver sa Place (Red Dirt Heart 4)

Le Poids de Sentiments (The Weight of It All)

Un Noël à la sauce Henry (A Very Henry Christmas)

Une vie à Refaire (Switched)

Evolution (Evolved)

Galaxies & Océans

Qui Trouve, Garde (Finders Keepers)

Sens Dessus Dessous (Upside Down)

La Haine au Fond du Verre (The hate You Drink)

Tallowwood

Spencer Cohen Series

GERMAN

Flammende Erde (Red Dirt Heart)

Lodernde Erde (Red Dirt Heart 2)

Sengende Erde (Red Dirt Heart 3)

Ungezähmte Erde (Red Dirt Heart 4)

Vier Pfoten und ein bisschen Zufall (Finders Keepers)

Ein Kleines bisschen Versuchung (The Weight of It All)

Ein Kleines Bisschen Fur Immer (A Very Henry Christmas)

Weil Leibe uns immer Bliebt (Switched)

Drei Herzen eine Leibe (Three's Company)

Über uns die Sterne, zwischen uns die Liebe (Galaxies and Oceans)

Unnahbares Herz (Blind Faith 1)

Sehendes Herz (Blind Faith 2)

Hoffnungsvolles Herz (Blind Faith 3)

Verträumtes Herz (Blind Faith 3.5)

Thomas Elkin: Verlangen in neuem Design

Thomas Elkin: Leidenschaft in klaren

Thomas Elkin: Vertrauen in bester Lage

Traummann töpfern leicht gemacht (Throwing Hearts)

Sir

THAI

Sixty Five Hours (Thai translation)

Finders Keepers (Thai translation)

SPANISH

Sesenta y Cinco Horas (Sixty Five Hours)

Los Doce Días de Navidad

Código Rojo (Code Red)

Código Azul (Code Blue)

Queridísimo Milton James

Queridísimo Malachi Keogh

El Peso de Todo (The Weight of it All)

Tres Muérdagos en Raya: Serie Navidad en Hartbridge

Lista De Deseos Navideños: Serie Navidad en Hartbridge

Feliz Navidad Cupido: Serie Navidad en Hartbridge

Spencer Cohen Libro Uno

Spencer Cohen Libro Dos

Spencer Cohen Libro Tres

Davo

Hasta la Luna y de Vuelta

CHINESE

Blind Faith

JAPANESE

Bossy